Titles by *Langaa*

Francis B. Nyamnjoh
Stories from Abakwa
Mind Searching
The Disillusioned African
The Convert
Souls Forgotten
Married But Available

Dibussi Tande
No Turning Back. Poems of Freedom 1990-1993
Scribbles from the Den: Essays on Politics and Collective Memory in Cameroon

Kangsen Feka Wakai
Fragmented Melodies

Ntemfac Ofege
Namondo. Child of the Water Spirits
Hot Water for the Famous Seven

Emmanuel Fru Doh
Not Yet Damascus
The Fire Within
Africa's Political Wastelands: The Bastardization of Cameroon
Oriki'badan
Wading the Tide

Thomas Jing
Tale of an African Woman

Peter Wuteh Vakunta
Grassfields Stories from Cameroon
Green Rape: Poetry for the Environment
Majunga Tok: Poems in Pidgin English
Cry, My Beloved Africa
No Love Lost
Straddling The Mungo: A Book of Poems in English & French

Ba'bila Mutia
Coils of Mortal Flesh

Kehbuma Langmia
Titabet and the Takumbeng
An Evil Meal of Evil

Victor Elame Musinga
The Barn
The Tragedy of Mr. No Balance

Ngessimo Mathe Mutaka
Building Capacity: Using TEFL and African Languages as Development-oriented Literacy Tools

Milton Krieger
Cameroon's Social Democratic Front: Its History and Prospects as an Opposition Political Party, 1990-2011

Sammy Oke Akombi
The Raped Amulet
The Woman Who Ate Python
Beware the Drives: Book of Verse

Susan Nkwentie Nde
Precipice
Second Engagement

Francis B. Nyamnjoh & Richard Fonteh Akum
The Cameroon GCE Crisis: A Test of Anglophone Solidarity

Joyce Ashuntantang & Dibussi Tande
Their Champagne Party Will End! Poems in Honor of Bate Besong

Emmanuel Achu
Disturbing the Peace

Rosemary Ekosso
The House of Falling Women

Peterkins Manyong
God the Politician

George Ngwane
The Power in the Writer: Collected Essays on Culture, Democracy & Development in Africa

John Percival
The 1961 Cameroon Plebiscite: Choice or Betrayal

Albert Azeyeh
Réussite scolaire, faillite sociale : généalogie mentale de la crise de l'Afrique noire francophone

Aloysius Ajab Amin & Jean-Luc Dubois
Croissance et développement au Cameroun : d'une croissance équilibrée à un développement équitable

Carlson Anyangwe
Imperialistic Politics in Cameroun: Resistance & the Inception of the Restoration of the Statehood of Southern Cameroons
Betrayal of Too Trusting a People: The UN, the UK and the Trust Territory of the Southen Cameroons

Bill F. Ndi
K'Cracy, Trees in the Storm and Other Poems
Map: Musings On Ars Poetica
Thomas Lurting: The Fighting Sailor Turn'd Peaceable / Le marin combattant devenu paisible

Kathryn Toure, Therese Mungah Shalo Tchombe & Thierry Karsenti
ICT and Changing Mindsets in Education

Charles Alobwed'Epie
The Day God Blinked

G. D. Nyamndi
Babi Yar Symphony
Whether losing, Whether winning
Tussles: Collected Plays
Dogs in the Sun

Samuel Ebelle Kingue
Si Dieu était tout un chacun de nous ?

Ignasio Malizani Jimu
Urban Appropriation and Transformation: bicycle, taxi and handcart operators in Mzuzu, Malawi

Justice Nyo' Wakai
Under the Broken Scale of Justice: The Law and My Times

John Eyong Mengot
A Pact of Ages

Ignasio Malizani Jimu
Urban Appropriation and Transformation: Bicycle Taxi and Handcart Operators

Joyce B. Ashuntantang
Landscaping and Coloniality: The Dissemination of Cameroon Anglophone Literature

Jude Fokwang
Mediating Legitimacy: Chieftaincy and Democratisation in Two African Chiefdoms

Michael A. Yanou
Dispossession and Access to Land in South Africa: an African Perspevctive

Tikum Mbah Azonga
Cup Man and Other Stories

John Nkemngong Nkengasong
Letters to Marions (And the Coming Generations)

Amady Aly Dieng
Les étudiants africains et la littérature négro-africaine d'expression française

Tah Asongwed
Born to Rule: Autobiography of a life President

Frida Menkan Mbunda
Shadows From The Abyss

Bongasu Tanla Kishani
A Basket of Kola Nuts

Fo Angwafo III S.A.N of Mankon
Royalty and Politics: The Story of My Life

Basil Diki
The Lord of Anomy

Churchill Ewumbue-Monono
Youth and Nation-Building in Cameroon: A Study of National Youth Day Messages and Leadership Discourse (1949-2009)

Emmanuel N. Chia, Joseph C. Suh & Alexandre Ndeffo Tene
Perspectives on Translation and Interpretation in Cameroon

Linus T. Asong
The Crown of Thorns
No Way to Die
A Legend of the Dead: Sequel of *The Crown of Thorns*
The Akroma File

Vivian Sihshu Yenika
Imitation Whiteman

Beatrice Fri Bime
Someplace, Somewhere
Mystique: A Collection of Lake Myths

Shadrach A. Ambanasom
Son of the Native Soil
The Cameroonian Novel of English Expression: An Introduction

Tangie Nsoh Fonchingong and Gemandze John Bobuin
Cameroon: The Stakes and Challenges of Governance and Development

Tatah Mentan
Democratizing or Reconfiguring Predatory Autocracy? Myths and Realities in Africa Today

Roselyne M. Jua & Bate Besong
To the Budding Creative Writer: A Handbook

Albert Mukong
Prisonner without a Crime: Disciplining Dissent in Ahidjo's Cameroon

Mbuh Tennu Mbuh
In the Shadow of my Country

The Akroma File

Linus T. Asong

Langaa Research & Publishing CIG
Mankon, Bamenda

Publisher:
Langaa RPCIG
Langaa Research & Publishing Common Initiative Group
P.O. Box 902 Mankon
Bamenda
North West Region
Cameroon
Langaagrp@gmail.com
www.langaa-rpcig.net

Distributed outside N. America by African Books Collective
orders@africanbookscollective.com
www.africanbookscollective.com

Distributed in N. America by Michigan State University Press
msupress@msu.edu
www.msupress.msu.edu

ISBN: 9956-558-82-6

First Published in 1996 by Patron Publishing House,
Bamenda, Cameroon

Contents

For A Dear Sister, Mrs. Julie Fuoching

Whose Love, Patience and Tolerance

Helped Me Immensely

During the Period of Research for the Writing of

this Book.

Part One

Chapter One

(Saturday, April 21st, 1984)

The visitors had chosen the most appropriate hour to visit Reverend Mot Tomlinson. As a habit, two o'clock on Saturday afternoons was thirty minutes after lunch, and an hour to siesta time. That was when he read his weekend magazines and newspapers. He had just finished reading through the *DAILY GRAPHIC* and was reaching for *THE GHANAIAN TIMES* when he thought he heard a vehicle drive up to his gate and stop.

"Achampong," he called his house-boy.

"Pastor," the man answered from the kitchen and then hurried to the door into the parlour.

"See who is there," the Pastor said and, placing the newspaper on his laps, sank back in his lounge chair.

Achampong did not pass through the parlour. He went back towards the kitchen, passed through the back door and looked at the main gate from the back yard. He then returned through the same route, cleaned his feet on the door carpet into the parlour and announced:

"Two people, Pastor. An old man and a young man."

"What do they want?"

"I don't know, Pastor."

"Do you know them?"

"I think I have seen the old man here before, Pastor," the man said.

Reverend Mot Tomlinson motioned to him to go away, which he did. He then waited until he heard somebody fidgeting with the veranda gate. He rose and walked lackadaisically to the window, pulled the curtain to the right and looked out. The visitors were no strangers to him. The old man was Koto Thompson Akroma, the only Ghanaian who had been kind enough to allow the Lord of Israel Church of Evangelization (LICE) to settle on his land. The younger gentleman was his son Patrickston Essuman who Mot Tomlinson knew very well.

Why had they come, he wondered. Worry lines rose and implanted themselves on Mot Tomlinson's face like clouds foretelling a heavy down pour. Could it be that Akroma had been finally forced by his people to evict him? Where would LICE go to from Ghana?

"Achampong," he called his boy again.

"Open the gate and show them where to sit," he said when the man came again from behind the house. He then sat up in his chair and reflected on the past of the organisation which he now headed.

2

The Right Reverend Mot Tomlinson had begun his missionary activities as a Southern Baptist in a small church near the University of Chicago campus in the United States of America. His first trip to Africa had been in the company of the famous Reverend Carroll Webster, the first Christian to infiltrate the ranks of President Idi Amin's army with the teachings of the Gospel. That was in 1972. When Amin seized power, he needed money, and the only people who could readily do him the favour were the Arabs. He made overtures of friendliness to Colonel Ghadafi of Libya and King Faisal of Saudi Arabia.

In either case he was informed that the only thing demanded of him was a declaration of Moslem as the state religion of Uganda. That, by implication, meant the immediate elimination of all other religions, especially the Christian religions. To satisfy his benefactor, Amin went to the ridiculous extent of asking Pastors to cross out any mention of Israel from Bible readings over the national radio and other public prayer sessions.

In 1974, Amin banned all Christian religions, something he repeated in 1977. That year the Americans caused to be formed **Lord of Israel Church of Evangelisation** of which Mot Tom was appointed a leading member. The idea behind the creation of the church was to tease Amin into exhibiting his cruelty towards minority religions and so justify an eventual overthrow through the combined efforts of the churches and the Western powers.

The ploy worked. As had been expected, President Idi Amin found the name so provocative that he put out a special squad to wipe the organisation from the surface of the earth. That year, Mot Tom escaped to Ghana from whence the church began to spread its influence across West and Central Africa. The most conducive atmosphere in which it thrived was under repressive regimes, the main idea behind its existence being to test the tolerance of Governments in which the Western powers did not have much confidence.

3

As soon as Achampong reported that the guests had sat down and were expecting him, Mot Tom opened the door and went out to meet them.

"When I see you at this hour after such a long time Mr. Akroma, I am worried. Is there a problem?"

"There is," the old man answered gravely, looking from his son to the Pastor. Mot Tom took in a long breath of uneasiness and leaned forward to listen. To his greatest relief, what the old man said had little to do with what he had feared.

He recounted Ghana's tribulations since the overthrow of Nkrumah in Ghana. The coming of Jerry Rawlings and what he described as his "short-sighted" economic policies, he said, had brought relief to some quarters and much pain and suffering to others. In particular, he drew attention to Rawling's recent cancellation of national debts incurred by the previous regime, on grounds that the monies had not been used for the benefit of the ordinary Ghanaian tax-payer, an act which had endeared Rawlings to the common man.

His son, Essuman Patrickston, he said, had been awarded a scholarship by the Belgian government. He was still putting together his dossiers for travelling when the declaration was made. Since Belgium was one of Ghana's major creditors, in retaliation, she cancelled scholarships already promised. Akroma junior could therefore not leave the country.

Rawling's second decree, he said, hurt the Akroma family immensely. In a bid to please the populace Rawlings' decree decided the price of essential commodities, placing them at the reach of everybody. At that rate they could not sell enough to pay back their debts.

"I owed Central Bank of Ghana 35,000 New Cedis," he went on. "The bank insists that we continue to pay the sum of 1000 New Cedis every quarter, or else we shall lose our land, including this land on which we are sitting now and talking."

"So how can LICE be of help, Mr. Akroma? You need a loan or something?" Reverend Mot Tomlinson inquired.

It was the young man who responded. He told Reverend Mot Tomlinson that anything should be done to make him leave the country and live in the Franc zone, like Togo, for about a year. During that time he would be able to raise money, convert it in the black market, into Ghanaian New Cedis. That way he would be able to pay back the loan.

Inadvertently, Akroma Senior harped Mot Tomlinson's fears aright by reminding him over and over of how much sacrifice his family had made on behalf of LICE, "If not of this my family," he said, "this your church would never have settled in Ghana, especially as you came just when we were hearing in the papers, radio and television of the Jones Town Massacre in Guyana in 1979"

Reverend Mot Tomlinson nodded.

"You know how much we have had to put up against our people in Accra here," he went on. "We have actually not got anything for what we did except that our people only laugh at me. This is the very first favour we are asking LICE."

Reverend Mot Tomlinson blinked nervously.

"I don't think we have ever done anything to make you think we are ungrateful for what you did to LICE, Mr. Akroma," he said.

"I know," the old man said.

"I just wish you could ask me another favour," Reverend Mot Tomlinson said regretfully. "Any other favour," he repeated. "I find it difficult to solve this problem," he confessed.

The old man shook his head sadly and grinned. "You do all this to somebody," he seemed to say to himself "and the very first time you ask for a favour, he wants to tell you what to ask for!"

Reverend Mot Tom's left hand rose to his mouth. He squeezed his lower lip tight for a long time as his eyes moved from the old man to his son and back. He saw clearly that this was the one opportunity to show his appreciation for the services rendered them to his church. He resolved to help, somehow.

"Give me some time to think about it," he told them. "Even if I do not solve it the way you are thinking, there may yet be some other way out."

Chapter Two

(Monday, April 23rd, 1984)

Reverend Mot Tomlinson was not only the Moderator of LICE International in the Greater Accra Region, he was also the current chairman of LICE in West and Central Africa. Since receiving the odious request from the Akromas, he spent many of the waking hours of the night trying to figure out possibilities of showing his gratitude to that family for standing so solidly behind his church.

After lunch on Monday he drove to the Akroma residence which he knew so well at Okyema Circle. The entire Akroma family was glad to see him. Very expectantly, sons, daughters, grandchildren and close relatives ran and came to greet him. It was certain that they were all aware of the family problem and the fact that the only solution laid with Mot Tomlinson.

After their greetings the elder Akroma dismissed them. As soon as they were together Mot Tomlinson said exactly what the old man wanted to hear.

"Ever since you brought up the problem the other day," he began, "I have done a lot of homework and I seem to have come up with some ideas. But I would like to have a few things clear in my mind. For how long does your son want to stay away? You talked only of the franc zone and mentioned Lome. Must it be only Togo? Could he not go anywhere else like to Nigeria or to Cameroon?"

"Essuman himself will answer that," the old man said and sent for his son who had been resting in a small room far behind the yard. When he came and Mot Tomlinson posed the questions he told him:

"Reverend, I said one year, but it will depend on how I make it out there."

On the question as to whether he could not go to Nigeria the old man said:

"Nigerians are just like us, British people, too honest, too straightforward, too well organised, too very strict. You cannot cause them to do things you want. They will catch you. They will not even allow you to enter. With the French people it is different.... We want a place where things look good but are scattered. It is easy to play tricks with them."

Both men smiled

"What exactly do you have in mind, should your son gain entry into any of those countries," he addressed the old man directly, "what do we expect that he will do to survive?"

"Pastor," the old man responded, "when a man is drowning, you cannot tell what he will hold to survive. But my son is a decent child. We are from a decent family," he ended up confidently, a good-natured smile playing on his serious parted lips.

He looked across at his son who reassured Reverend Pastor Mot Tomlinson: "Pastor, I am no criminal. The fact that we are so poor does not mean that we have to commit crimes. We have appealed to you because we think you can have an idea which appealed to you because we think you can have an idea which will not embarrass any anybody."

There was a long silence and then the young man asked:

"Why did you talk about Cameroon, Reverend?"

"Because I think we just missed an opportunity," Reverend Mot Tomlinson said.

"Opportunity, Reverend?"

Reverend Mot Tomlinson nodded and said:

"There was supposed to be an Episcopal Seminar of *LICE International* of the West and Central Africa in Cameroon from the 14th through the 18th of May. It has been cancelled because of the political crisis there now. When it comes up again, we should be able to smuggle you into the team…"

Essuman reflected for some time and the asked:

"When is the next one, Reverend?"

"As I said, it is not certain, and it may not actually be in Cameron. It is possible that it will take place in some French-speaking country. As a matter of fact, my colleague in Cameroon has suggested Togo, Chad, Guinea and the like."

Essuman was a young man who thought out things very fast. He pulled at is beard pensively for no longer than one minute and then said: "Reverend, in my mind I think all is not yet lost."

Reverend Mot Tomlinson looked levelly at him.

"How do you mean?" he inquired.

"Suppose we pretend that you did not hear about the cancellation or postponement…?"

"And then?"

"And then you send me there as a member of the team? I just want to get into Cameroon, Reverend. I have heard so much about the place as a country of endless opportunities of survival, a place where only fools suffer."

2

On Tuesday Reverend Mot Tomlinson invited Essuman Patrickston Akroma to whom he read two letters he had carefully prepared. The first and by far the more important, was addressed to a certain Reverend Dieudonne Akwa. Essuman held his head down and could feel a tear run down his cheek. He was weeping for joy.

"How could Pastor come up with such an idea." He exclaimed.

"Pastor is a human being like you," the man beamed.

"That is precisely what I need, Reverend," Essuman said gratefully. "I will never forget this," And then looking at the second letter he inquired: "Who is this Pastor Dieudonne, if I may ask?"

"Reverend Dieudonne Akwa is the Moderator for the Littoral, the host and convener of the supposed Seminar."

"Thank you very sincerely," Essuman said. "My old man will be very glad to hear this."

"You are welcome," Reverend Mot Tomlinson said.

"We have been looking for an opportunity to show how grateful we are to your family. This is our first chance."

He then stretched the second letter. It was addressed to the Immigration Officer at the Douala airport. It merely introduced Essuman to the authorities as a representative of LICE International of Ghana.

"This is the letter you will use to obtain your passport and exit visa here in Accra," he told Essuman. "The letter to Reverend Akwa must be delivered to him directly, personally as soon as you meet him at the Douala airport. You must do so discreetly because it will blow the whole thing up if it falls into the hands of the airport authorities."

Chapter Three

(Douala International Airport, Monday, May 7th 1984)

Because of the dubious circumstances surrounding his travel plans, Essuman Patrickson Akroma's departure from Ghana remained a closely guarded secret known only to Reverend Mot Tomlinson, his father and a few relatives. He left Kotoka International Airport for Cameroon at eight o'clock on Monday the 7th of May, 1984, by an Air Afrique plane.

After brief stops at Cotonu, Lagos and Calabar, the plane touched down at the Douala International Airport at precisely three o'clock. It was a far cry from what he had left behind either in the Kotoka International Airport in Accra or the Mutala Mohammed International Airport in Lagos. Although he had been too worried to notice it, there was much in the plane that had brought him to prepare his mind for what to expect.

Seat numbers and positions had been carefully indicated on the Air tickets. It was also indicated on the tickets whether the holder required the smoking or non-smoking compartment. But once they got into the plane nobody seemed to care about the positions and numbers of the tickets. Smokers even left the non-smoking compartments to ask for cigarette lighters from the general compartments. Passengers only stopped smoking when they ran out of cigarettes. At the take off they continued to smoke even when the warning sign was given to fasten seat belts and put out cigarettes.

From Calabar Akroma noticed that seat belts were no longer necessary because seats meant for two passengers were occupied by four or more persons. Many passengers like him who had travelled from Accra lost their seats every time they rose. And because there was not enough room for the stewards to move up and down, there was no means of calling anybody to order.

There was more to interest him when the plane had finally come to a halt, the door thrown open and the staircase lowered. Only the runway looked completed and there was enough evidence all over the place that much more work still needed to be done. The entrance into the airport building from the plane was a truncated structure to which a tube was to have been connected to the plane such that passengers would move from the building to the plane and back without being seen from outside. The truncated tunnel of a corridor stood some two hundred metres away from the plan. It would be terrible if it rained because the airport would not protect anybody.

At first he thought it would be bad news for passengers who had several pieces of hand luggage, for they would have to make numerous trips to the plane. But he seemed to be the only person to bother about that. While they inched their way towards the tunnel he noticed that many of the police men patrolling the airport took bags from passengers and disappeared under the building. They would eventually reunite outside the building to settle their accounts, he thought. If he had come to Cameroon anxious to see what was repeatedly called "Advanced Democracy," there it was. People did whatever they wanted to do with impunity. The lady who cut the tickets from passengers alighting from the plane abandoned the exercise at one point because a passenger made a rude comment to her.

At one point he thought with inward amusement that the *Tro-Tros* that plied the roads in Ghana would do just as well in the air with only two wings and an engine. For, the plane was just as uncomfortable. The toilet door had been ripped open and left hanging on only one hinge, making it not only difficult to use the toilet but uncomfortable to sit at the rear. This, he thought, was the kind of place he needed. And there was more to please him!.

The corridor that led to the customs and police reception and inspection areas was littered with cigarette ends, bits and pieces of toilet tissue and even groundnut peelings, evidence that the cleaner may not have done his work for a long time. Half the police men on duty were carelessly dressed, with portions of their shirts flying over their trousers. The one thing they seemed to keep in place was the gun.

2

The Customs did not detain him much. He was no trader and did not like one, not even in disguise. Therefore, they were not look likely to gain anything from wasting time in searching him. As a matter of formality, however, they asked him to declare his money. All he could produce was one hundred New Cedis. That fetched him twenty-seven thousand eight hundred francs. And even if he had been a trader, he had just been shown how to solve the problem. A Moslem trader had just pulled out a bundled of notes and handed over to the Custom Inspector who had actually carried his bag through the rest of the barriers before returning to attend to them.

From the Customs he was supposed to move across to the Emi-Immigration desk. He did not do that. Instead he bent towards the *Brigadier des Douanes* who had just attended to him with a request:

"Can I use your toilet, please," he asked politely. "I think I have a running stomach."

"You bring shit from Ghana to shit in Cameroon?" the man who definitely had a wonderful sense of humour asked with a wry smile, puffing at his cigarette, blowing the smoke over his shoulders into the eyes and nostrils of passengers, not caring a thing about the nose twitching and sneezing that indicated their discomfort.

Akroma was in no mood to share in the joke.

3

Not quite ten metres away stood a police Inspector who looked very different from the rest of his kind. Kum Dangobert was his name but he was nicknamed Scotland Yard among his colleagues. He was so named not only because he was from the famous Mutengene Police College (also popularly called SCOTLAND YARD, on account of the rigorous training offered there) but because of his extraordinary powers of smelling crimes and unveiling them. For instance, he was the one who first suspected the famous Nyabekong Scandal involving a beautiful glob-trotter-of-a-girl who was eventually discovered to have been dealing in cocaine by transporting it, sewn into her calves. He was also the one who first suspected sewn into her calves. He was also the one who first suspected that the dead child from Kinshasa had gold sewn in its belly. There were many other stories circulating about his detective prowess, most of them true.

From a distance Dangobert had been watching him with inquisitive suspicion, with a rising of the loathing he felt for all Ghanaians, a loathing which was actually physical, as at the approach of some noisome and disgusting creature, full of venom and noxiousness. The fact that Akroma was from Ghana, coupled with his seemingly harmless request and the Customs Officer's joke drew his attention.

4

His suspicion of Ghanaians, however, was not based on any firsthand experience with the latter. It grew from stories told by people who had studied in Ghana and those who had lived with Ghanaians abroad. There was, for instance, his uncle who worked at the Cameroon Embassy at Ottawa, and who told him each time he came home that Ghanaians were always at the centre of most of the problems African students caused in Canada.

There was a very painful story he told of one Ansu Techema, a Ghanaian who had been voted the president of the International Students Association in 1974, an association which was dominated by African students in Canada. The story went that upon arrival in Canada, Techema applied to become a landed Immigrant. The procedure was so complicated that his application was rejected. He later learned that if he got married to a Canadian, that would make things easier for him. Within a few months he got himself a Canadian girl, Farrar Bronowsky, to whom he got married, even though he had left his legally married wife back in Kumasi in Ghana.

Techema never mentioned his first marriage to Farrar. Techema and Farrar eventually had a baby boy. When the boy was getting to a year old Techema began to feel a strong need to bring his Ghanaian wife over to Canada to improve on her education. To succeed he told Farrar that he would like the boy to grow up according to strict Ghanaian customs. This, he said could only work if they arranged for a baby-sitter to be sent to them from Ghana.

Farrar agreed and within two months a baby-sitter arrived from Ghana. Her name was Evelyn Ablavi, his own wife. One month after Ablavi's arrival, Farrar was said to have thrown herself to her death through the window of their six-storey apartment, during a domestic disagreement. A case was made of it, but for want of sufficient evidence to incriminate him, Techema was eventually acquitted. But the African Community which was aware of what Techema had done, was so outraged that it voted him out of the office of President of the International Students. That however, did not change Techema's status as a Landed Immigrant, which was what was important to him and Ablavi.

There were also stories of Ghanaians who had been arrested trying to smuggle large quantities of gold and diamond across the border, in the bellies of corpses. All these and many more had permanently tainted Dangobert's view of Ghanaians. He always remembered what his uncle said repeatedly; "Never trust a Ghanaian, even if he is dead!"

Chapter Four

(Wednesday, May 9th 1984)

When Akroma obtained permission to go to the toilet, the Customs Officer did not object, in spite of the expensive joke that he cracked.

"Feel free," he said, pointing to the corridor that led to the place. The visitor picked up his large green 1984 diary and walked into the toilet and locked the door behind him. The Inspector was following him with his eyes.

Although he merely wanted to ensure that he made no mistake, Essuman actually felt the urge to go to stool. As he sat on the toilet bowl he took out the two letters and separated them to make sure that he did not give the police the wrong one. He pulled out the letter to Reverend Akwa and looked at the address. The envelope bore the label CONFIDENTIAL on the top centre. To the top left hand corner it bore the name of the sender.

Reverend Mot Tomlinson
LICE International, Accra- Ghana.

There was a wash-hand basin on the wall directly in front of him. The toilet room was so small that he could even turn the tap on and off from the sitting position. He stretched the letter and placed it between the sink and an iron bar that supported the basin. He stuck the letter to the police between clasped lips.

He rubbed his face with his hands and looked at the letter to the police, which he looked at again as if to reassure himself of some fact.

As he groaned to relieve himself he heard a knock at the door, followed by the question:

"Who's in there?" from outside.

"Me," the passenger answered.

"You who?"

"Essuman Akroma, please," he said.

"Have you been inspected at the Emi-Immigration?"

"Not yet, sir."

"Hurry up, then," the voice ordered.

Akroma's intestines seemed to freeze instantly and he finished up in a hurry, prematurely. He then flushed the toilet and walked out. The Inspector of Police who had trailed him with his eyes was standing at the door. The man waited until the visitor had picked up his luggage and had begun to move in the direction of the Immigration desk. Instead of receiving him at the desk as he had received the other guests, the Inspector led Akroma into the office of the *Commissaire*. This made the visitor exceeding uneasy.

2

The two men walked in without knocking at the door and handed the letter to the *Commissaire.* The man tore it open and read:

To Whom It May Concern.

This is to certify that the bearer of this letter - Patrickston Essuman Akroma is the representative of the Greater Accra Region at the 11th Episcopal Seminar of LICE (Lord of Israel Church of Evangelization) International, scheduled to take place in Douala from the 14th through the 18th of May, 1984.

Contact man in Cameroon: Reverend Dieudonne Akwa LICE International, Littoral Head Office.

P.O Box 6295
Bonandjo, Douala
Cameroon.

The *Commissaire* studied the letter for a while and asked:

"Where is your return ticket?"

Essuman pulled it out of his diary and handed over to the *Commissaire*. The man looked at it but without visible concern. Dangobert looked at the visitor for a while and then suggested to his chief:

"Let's telephone his host, Chief."

The *Commissaire* nodded and told him:

"Get him on the line for me."

The Inspector immediately picked up the Telephone Directory from a shelf behind him and ran his fingers through the pages until he came to the Douala section. He then ran his eyes down the L column until he came to LICE. He noted down the phone number, closed the directory and dialled.

Akroma bit his left index fingernail briefly and breathed in and out sharply as he sized him up quickly. He was above average in height, looking even taller than Akroma who was himself very tall. But he was more muscular, with a plump face and although he may not have been older than Akroma by much, he had gone slightly bald on the forehead and on the temples. He had two large stick-out ears that strangely enough seemed to move as he spoke or raised his brows. A long scar ran from just below the corner of his left eye to the base of the left cheekbone. There were two smaller ones on his forehead, one descending into his thick brows and the other rising into his bald head. This was more than enough testimony that he could very well have grappled with a lion, and could very well do so again.

Something in his lips and eyes frightened Akroma: his mouth and eyes. His eyes were expressive, sharp, penetrating and investigative as they rolled behind his steel-rimmed glasses. Akroma thought the man probably knew that the eyes betrayed him, for he kept looking away from him. He had a large upper lip framed by a heavy moustache that stretched from one corner of the mouth to the other. His lower lip was thin and he seemed to gnaw at it constantly as though he was suppressing some hidden but acute fury. At the end of his huge arms were two relatively small fingers and hands which Akroma found strangely delicate.

His voice was husky and he seemed to clear his throat several times when he spoke. If as he had once learned from his Theosophy Classes, "The body (indeed) bears the imprint of the inner forces which animate it," then Inspector Kum Dangobert was certainly not the kind of people he would like to meet on such a mission as delicate as the one he had embarked on. And events will prove him right!.

3

"Is that the residence of the Moderator of the Lord of Israel Church of Evangelization?"

Akroma cocked his ears and heard the policeman inquire.

"Yes, it is," a deep sonorous and rather impatient voice answered and then immediately asked: "Who is talking?"

Kum Dangobert, Inspector of Police, Emi-Immigration, Douala International Airport."

There was a rather long pause at the other end of the line before the voice asked:

"Who?" he inquired again.

Dangobert did not answer. He instead handed over the receiver to his boss. The *Commissaire* asked:

"Can I talk to Reverend Pastor Dieudonne Akwa?"

"You are talking to Reverend Dieudonne Akwa," the voice said. "Who is it?"

Akroma shifted his weight from the left to the right foot and looked at the *Commissaire* and the Inspector, his eyes blinking nervously and copiously.

"Yves Tourne Cocons, *Commissaire* for Emi-Immigration, Douala International Airport."

There was a brief silence. The man at the other end coughed dryly and asked with obvious bewilderment in his voice. "Excuse me, sir, whom am I talking to? Is it the Inspector or the *Commissaire*..."

"The *Commissaire* for Emi-Immigration asked Inspector Dangobert to get the Moderator of LICE on the line. This is the *Commissaire* speaking now, does that make sense?"

"Now it does?"

"Can I, therefore, speak to the Moderator?" the *Commissaire* asked. His voice was authoritative but not harsh and he did not talk as if he had anything against Ghanaians.

"This is the Moderator speaking, Monsieur Le *Commissaire*. Reverend Dieudonne Akwa. What can I do for you?"

4

It was at this point that Akroma looked at him more critically. He was a lot older than the Inspector but looked a bit timid and benignant, not too sure of himself. He looked a lot easier to deal with than the monster-of-an-Inspector who scared him so badly. Akroma looked at his shoulder. He was wearing five stars, good reason why he did not seem to bother himself as much as the Inspector. Unless it came soon, he may never add another star before retiring from service. He behaved like the kind of old civil servant who wants to play safe, who wants to go about his work as unperturbed as possible until the day came when he would leave the service and wait for death. Clasping his walkie-talkie under his left armpit he held the telephone receiver in his right hand and inquired:

"Do you know a certain Reverend Mot To-To –Tom-Lison…," the *Commissaire* inquired with stiff formality.

"You mean Reverend Mot Tomlinson?" Akwa asked.

"Yes," the *Commissaire* said. "Reverend Mot Tomlison of Accra."

"I know him," Akwa said. "That's our Moderator in the Greater Accra Region of Ghana. He's my colleague. Any problem, Monsieur Le *Commissaire*?"

"Pastor," the *Commissaire* began, sending the mercury of Akroma's anxiety soaring into the ceiling. "I am calling about a certain visitor from Accra. His name is Patrickston Essuman Akroma. He is said to be coming for a certain Episcopal Seminar of LICE International, which he says is supposed to last from the 14th to the 18th of this May. He is carrying a letter from Reverend Mot Tomlinson in Ghana.

We need confirmation from you to let him in. Are you aware of the seminar?"

There was an unnecessary pause and Reverend Akwa admitted: "I am aware of the seminar." He wanted to add that the seminar had been cancelled, but he changed his mind. There was no doubt that the seminar had been cancelled. Was he going to turn away a participant so bluntly? Perhaps the information on the cancellation had not reached Ghana.

Telephone lines to the outside world had been cut immediately following the abortive coup of April 6th, 1984. He had sent letters to various zones announcing the cancellation, and so he was anxious to know what was going on in Ghana and the neighbouring zones. He would admit the visitor, if only to get news from Ghana.

The *Commissaire* announced to Akroma:

"You are allowed into the country for up to 25 days. Can you find your way to Pastor Akwa's residence?" he asked.

"I have never been here before," Akroma said with visible relief.

The *Commissaire* who had not dropped the line said again: "Are you there, Reverend?"

"Listening," Akwa answered with a trace of impatience. He hated having anything to do with the police.

"Your visitor does not know his way about. Are you coming for him or you will send somebody?'

"I will send my driver," Reverend Akwa said and immediately dropped the line. The *Commissaire* stamped the passport and returned to him.

"They are coming for you," he said and showed the visitor his way out of the immigration section. "Enjoy your stay in Cameroon," he said. He seemed to be just as relieved as Akroma. The visitor thanked him and walked out. It looked so easy, so unbelievably effortless to enter Cameroon. All the omens must be in favour of his mission, he concluded.

Chapter Five

(Wednesday, May 9th 1984)

It must have been one full hour after Akroma left the *Commissaire*'s office when he saw a man through the naked window louvers of the Arrivals Passengers' lounge. He was coming up the steps into the airport and inquiring something from the little groups of people on the veranda and corridor.

Akroma's instincts told him that he must be Reverend Akwa's driver. He was unusually thin and had features which but for the dark skin, would pass for an Ethiopian or some Fulani individual. In fact, the man reminded Akroma of some cattle rearers in Tamale or the extreme northern part of Ghana. His head was longish, rather than oval as that of the rest of the people around. His chin was also long, adorned with a dark unkempt goatee of a beard.

The rest of his face was bare except for scanty whiskers. His neck was long and thin, with a rather pronounced Adam's apple. His hands were thin and long with thin fingers, brown, indicating that he was a very heavy smoker. This initial guess was confirmed when he smiled, betraying two rows of badly disfigured teeth.

He may not have been older than Akroma by much, although his features looked hardened, more from labour, and toil, perhaps, than age. His forehead was harshly lined and his jaw-bone high and protruding. He was wearing a coat and a tie with the shirt buttoned so far down that his swan-like neck gave the impression of an under-nourished gentleman.

As Akroma still stood watching he saw Inspector Dangobert appear from another corner of the building and walk down to the man and question him briefly. He saw the new-comer take out something from his pocket and show the Inspector who studied it for a while before returning it to him. He then went back to his hiding place.

Akroma then walked to the man and asked: "Are you looking for a visitor from Ghana?"

"Yes, Oga. Rev. Nkrumah…"

"No, not Nkrumah, Akroma," the visitor corrected the man.

"Yes, Oga. Pastor Akwa sent me. I am the driver. Mombangui Jean-Paul is my name. They always call me only J.P. Even nearly everybody call me J-P. I come from Small Monje. I am a freeborn of Biongong, but I live and work here. I have been working with Pastor Akwa for many years."

Akroma looked at the man and smiled and remained silent. Was it necessary to be introducing himself to drivers, especially to a man who was ready to say so much about himself unprovoked, and in one breath?

J-P took the bag from him, and seemed so eager to serve that he even asked to carry the visitor's diary.

"Don't worry, I will hold this myself," Akroma said. J-P walked ahead of his guest towards a waiting SUBARU. He walked with unbalanced steps and seemed to have knocked knees. His entire weight seemed to rest on his heels and one could see his finger-like toes, one almost on top of the other rubbing against each other in the sandals he wore.

"Do you live far from here?" Akroma asked. "I have been waiting for over an hour since I called."

"Not too far, Oga". J-P said, "Only say amboutillage, is hab die."

Akroma did not answer. He did not understand what the man said. J-P put the bag in the trunk, opened the back door for the guest and waited until he had settled in his boss' seat. He then shut the door firmly, walked round and entered.

2

He put on his seat belt, adjusted the driving mirror and threw a quick glance at the visitor's face. It was a study in frightful concentration, hard, dry and expressionless, slashed by a pair of cold thick lips on which a smile may find it hard to settle. He had large sleepy eyes set wide apart. His eyelids were heavy, beneath which glowed a piercing severe glare. Akroma had large sleepy eyes set wide apart. His spongy hair grew thickly on his head but ended far above his large protruding forehead.

"Oga is visiting?" J-P asked in a polite voice as they drove out of the airport grounds.

"Yes," Akroma answered and looked through the window. Inspector Dangobert had already returned to the veranda and was pacing up and down, his baton clasped in both hands behind his back. He said nothing else to J-P. For about thirty minutes they drove in silence while Akroma just kept making notes in his diary, combining and cancelling strategies in his mind. He was glad to be in Cameroon and did not want to waste any minute. It looked so easy, getting in there. His mind was considering options. He would be a hair-dresser, he would be a cook in a hotel, a photographer, a private instructor for homes, a fake insurance broker, a money-doubler, a pimp, a business consultant, a public letter writer, a taxi-man, a teacher in a private college, or all of the above. He would do anything that would fetch him money.

Chapter Six

(Wednesday, May 9th 1984)

Around the month of May the weather in Douala could be very inconstant. When J-P left the house there was abundant sunshine. By the time he arrived the airport it started drizzling. When they got into the car to drive away it actually began to pour, and it got progressively worse as they drove on, making the journey extremely slow. Here a taxi overtook and suddenly stopped to pick up a passenger, there another hooted only to stop just when you were about to make way for him to pass.

Because of the bad weather Akroma was not able to get a good view of the town he had come to explore. He decided it was poor strategy to sit back instead of finding our as much as possible even before he settled down.

"About how large is this city?" he asked J-P.

"Ah-ah, Oga," the man beamed, "you cannot count Douala. It is a whole country. More than two million."

It was an exaggeration, but it gave the visitor an idea of the size.

"What kind of things do people do here to get money?"

"Oga, anything you do in Douala you have money. Even those who carry only shit in the night."

"How is business life there?"

"That is the worst. Every businessman is a millionaire."

"Is life cheap?"

"Like in what, Oga? Rent or chop or clothes?"

"Yes, something like that."

"It can be cheap if you want cheap things. For clothes, you can buy everything second-hand. Even shoes, socks, dross, tie, coat. All this that I am wearing, not up to 2,000 francs. Rent is also not very dear. You can get a one room house for 8,000francs like my own. Many many people do not live in houses...."

"Then how do they live?'

"They work and go to the bar and drink and dance and sit there until the next day, then they start again. Anything can happen in Douala. Only a foolish man can suffer in Douala."

2

It took them exactly one hour thirty minutes to make the tedious bumper-to-bumper journey of less than ten kilometres to Mambanda-Bonaberi where Reverend Dieudonne Akwa lived. His abode also served as the main office of LICE. It was a large enclosed compound containing the large main house and two smaller adjoining ones. There were two equally smaller houses set apart from each other. Flowers of various species and colour adorned the front yard. There were coconut trees to the back very close to the wall with a kitchen garden to the left and right of the coconut trees.

The man who came to the veranda to welcome them was unmistakably the Pastor. Akroma had his eyes fixed on him as they approached the house. He was a man of middle height and about sixty years old and the one remarkable thing about him as Akroma discovered instantly was his genial look. Once on their way to Mambanda-Bonaberi he asked J-P.

"Tell me, what kind of man do I expect to meet?"

"You mean man like how, Oga?" J-P. asked.

"A kind man, wild, good, quiet, generous, selfish. Something like that."

J-P had told him unhesitatingly:

"Even God not good reach Pastor Akwa. He can give people food and die hungry. People from all over come and live only with him. He is the real God man."

That had given him much hope. And even now that he was looking at the man he was not disappointed. He had the built that was fashionable amongst pastors whose churches were sponsored from abroad: a roundish, bespectacled, clean-shaven face, a thick neck below folds of skin and looked like several chins, a large protruding belly and short thick arms with fingers so thick that they did not look like they could bend. He seemed to live very well. His hair was low and scanty. He was not exactly bald but the hair-line retreated far above his forehead. He had roundish eyes with thick folds of flesh hanging below which gave the impression to a casual observer that they were very large. They were seemingly magnified by the thick lenses of the heavy spectacles he wore. He looked virtually over the spectacles. He was wearing a bluish long-sleeved shirt with rubber bands fastened to the arm between the shoulder and the elbow to keep the shirt in place. It seemed slightly too big and the arms too long. Below the shirt was a brown pair of trousers which he buttoned and belted right above his navel thereby accentuating the curvature of his belly.

He might just have returned from his office or was preparing to leave the house, for he wore a pair of leather bedroom slippers. He received Akroma with a gentle smile that seemed to have been switched on and off. He even helped J-P take in one of the bags. He had another pair of spectacles in his pocket, probably for reading. The ones he wore showed evidence of mending on the right hand side of the frame. His brows were thick. His nose was long with small nostrils, made even smaller by the weight of the spectacles pressing on the flanges.

He had a thick patch of moustache that barely spanned the lower part of the bridge of the nose. His cheeks were large and bulging with two deep crevice-like lines descending like a pair of dividers from below the lower rims of the spectacles into the lower jaws.

The house was tastefully, but not elaborately furnished, an abode that correctly marked its occupants as quiet cultured people. Rather fastidious in taste they either had no children or they had all grown and left their parents. The latter was more likely. There were flowers of all species on the veranda and in the parlour.

3

He greeted his guest with a respectful bow and then took him in while the driver brought in the luggage from the car. He showed Akroma a seat by his side and rose and went to the fridge and took out a bottle of orange juice. He opened the cupboard and took out two glasses, served himself a glass and also served his guest.

Akroma accepted with thanks. Reverend Akwa inquired about his flight, about things in Ghana which he said, compared to Cameroon, must be like heaven. He spoke of corpses which he had personally seen hauled away in trucks, following the political disorders.

"Not exactly a heaven," Akroma said. "We in Ghana are still living the terrible consequences of Rawlings' accession to power. We didn't quite see corpses, except for those of Achampong, Akufo, Afrifa and the other army officers they were compelled to clear away to sit comfortably on the throne."

He then went on to paint a bleak picture of Ghana as he left it, in order to prepare the man's mind for the reasons to justify his coming to Cameroon.

4

Reverend Akwa's serious parted lips transformed into a smile in which the visitor saw friendliness. He immediately proceeded to inquire about his guest. Akroma introduced himself. He told him where he was born, how old he was, that he had a B.A. degree in Education from Cape Coast University and an M.A. in the teaching of Geography from the University of Legon.

Reverend Akwa inquired about what was uppermost in his mind – the activities of LICE in Ghana, Ivory Coast, Liberia, Sierra Leone and the other regions.

The Pastor was quick to notice that Akroma did not seem to be sufficiently informed about that. What saved the situation from degenerating into instant suspicion was the entrance of the Pastor's wife whom Akroma studied very fast. Her bulk and gait disturbed him. She was certainly taller than the husband and only a bit younger, with age lines that rose into her head scarf. A thin line of hair ran round the natural border of her hair. There was then a small hairless gap of about one and a half centimetres which made it look as though someone had carefully ran a razor blade round her head. They call hair of such characteristic, he would be told later, "*mbamba.*"

She too was wearing spectacles with lighter lenses and thinner frames. Her eyebrows descended obliquely from her broad forehead, giving her a severe bitchy look. Her nose was short, her mouth small and her lips thick. When she came closer Akroma noticed a tuff of hair on her chin. Her neck over which she wore a lace of white beads with a small cross attached to it. She was wearing the kind of down-reaching gown generally *called Kaba Ngundu*, a casual wear for old women. And which seemed to conceal her enormous bulk. But one could easily see that her breasts which filled the whole chest were abnormally large for they seemed to descend to a little below the line of her elbow where the hands of the dress ended. Her arms were large and flabby and she had thick and long fingers. She reminded Akroma very much of the mistress he served when he was only a boy and who did not only starve them but caused their master to strip them naked before caning them whenever she decided that they had committed an offence. Thus he ruled her out at once as a wicked women.

5

He would be proved wrong!

"You meet my wife, Grace" Akwa said half-rising and pointing with an open palm at her. She walked up to Akroma who had long made up his mind about her and shook his hand.

"Welcome," she said and was just about to retreat to a seat at the dining table at the corner when the pastor added;

"He is Mr. Eshuman Ankroma. He was coming for the cancelled Seminar. News of the postponement did not reach them, it seems."

"Poor soul," the woman said with genuine sympathy and greeted him again. "Welcome to Cameroon."

Akroma thanked her and sat back.

"Have you had something to eat?" she asked with greatest concern. "Let me fetch you something," she said before Akroma had time to answer.

"You are very welcome," Akwa repeated his wife's greeting as Akroma drained his glass. "Your coming here is a mighty relief for us here," he began to Akroma's greatest delight. Akroma sat up with a start as though he had not heard him well. He went on:

"With the 6th April Coup story and its aftermath of turbulence, we have been completely cut off from the rest of the world. There must be some mix-up! I think it is the good Lord who had caused you to come because we have been thinking of holding this seminar we missed instead in

Ghana. I am indeed surprised that Reverend Mot Tomlinson is unaware of our postponement of the Seminar. I wrote to all participating regions. Anyway I don't blame him. There has been such blackout on news from here."

Akroma did not interrupt the man. A few minutes later Mrs. Akwa re-emerged with a plate of pop-corn and fried groundnuts.

Chapter Seven

(Wednesday, May 9th 1984)

Akroma was generally not a very forgetful individual. But because of the crucial importance of the letter he had reminded himself several times about the instructions. When, therefore, he was sure that Reverend Dieudonne Akwa had finished talking he said:

"Reverend Mot Tomlinson knew that the seminar had been postponed. Reverend Mot Tomlinson received your correspondence concerning the postponement."

"He did?" Reverend Akwa's brows pulled together as he instantly assumed a look of utter astonishment and perplexity. He turned and peered into Akroma's face for the first time, surprise written on every line of his own face.

"That he did?"

"Yes, Reverend, he did?"

Akroma looked round the house, sat up, bent towards Akwa and said with much hesitation:

"In fact, Reverend, my coming here is not actually connected to the seminar. We are just using the seminar as an excuse to get in here."

Reverend Akwa looked at him as if doing so for the first time, supported his chin in his left hand and creased his brows.

Sensing some trouble Akroma hastened to clarify the point:

"Actually my trip here is a deal which Reverend Mot Tomlinson and my father worked out. I even have a confidential letter from him that should explain exactly why I have come."

He was talking and searching his breast pocket. He searched first the left and the right. The letter was not there. He searched the pockets of his trousers, no good. He opened his diary several times, but all in vain. He then began thrusting his hands frantically and nervously into all his pockets over and over. It was his anxiety that first attracted Akwa's attention and made him suspicious.

"Are you sure you did not leave it behind in Ghana?" Akwa asked, his eyes twitching at the corners ominously.

Akroma shook his head violently. He recalled Reverend Mot Tomlinson's words when he handed over the letter to him.

"This letter is your passport to Cameroon. If you lose it, you have only yourself to blame. Don't let anybody else but Reverend Dieudonne Akwa touch it."

"There's no way I'll lose such a thing, Reverend," Akroma had said. "I would rather lose my life."

"I hope it never comes to that," the Pastor had told him.

2

I could never have forgotten it, Reverend," he said

"It was so important. I had it with me even at the airport."

"Sure you did not by any chance give it to the Immigration?"

"I could never have done so, Reverend. That's my life. I made sure I had it with me. If they saw it they would never have allowed me in here."

"But what was it all about? Can't you give me an idea of what it contained?'

Akroma took his time and explained as carefully as he could the services that LICE International owed them in Accra in Ghana. "You will find all that thoroughly explained in the letter," he ended up.

A state of disturbing anxiety set in. Reverend Akwa looked obviously irritated by the story. "Reverend Mot Tomlinson is a man we all respect in the line of our responsibilities as leaders of the church here," he said. "I am surprised that he would condescend to do such a thing. We've had lots of problems with the government, and to have allowed us to practice while closing down other churches such as Jehovah witnesses was a great concession! They will not be our friends for long when they discover that we are helping illegal immigrants. Anyway, let's see the letter," he insisted, looking at him with practiced mistrust.

As Akroma searched his pockets nervously and fruitlessly Akwa asked: "Why don't we go back to the Immigration and inquire?"

"That will be suicide, Reverend," the visitor said. "If the letter is in the hands of the Police, then I shall just be giving myself up for deportation."

Akwa's attitude changed immediately. The deal itself as Akroma explained to him sounded odious enough and if he was ever to agree to do it, it would be mainly because Reverend Mot Tomlinson was a friend of long-standing. If he ever rendered such a service, it was to remain a secret. But now that the letter might have fallen into foreign hands, he would be considered an accomplice to some dirty business. Besides, even if the letter turned up, the fact that Akroma had treated it with such nonchalance indicated that he could not be trusted to keep the entire affair a secret.

He would have nothing to do with Akroma, he resolved, even if the letter were discovered. He would explain to Reverend Mot Tomlinson why he refused to be of help.

Chapter Eight

(Wednesday, May 9th 1984)

Reverend Dieudonne Akwa decided that Akroma would have to go back to Ghana, as soon as the opportunity presented itself. The reputation of his church was at stake, he resolved. He was convinced that Akroma was merely faking the story of the letter. The more he tried to persuade Akwa the more adamant and irritated the latter became. It was a weakness of Akwa's character that he hardly changed his view once he had formed an opinion about something or somebody.

He left Akroma searching for the letter and went into his room. Akroma could hear him dialling, though he was too far to hear what was being said. It would be better, Akwa thought, for the Immigration to discover that letter when Akroma was already on the plane heading for Ghana, than to drag down his reputation and that of his Church in mud.

2

Another flight was still being expected and so Coçons and his crew were still on duty.

"Can I come over and talk to you?" Akwa inquired.

"By all means," the *Commissaire* said.

An hour later Reverend Akwa arrived the airport. It was Dangobert that he met first. Initially he did not want to discuss the matter with anybody else except the Police Chief. But Dangobert pressed on, telling him that it was he who made the call to Akwa's house. Reverend Akwa then told him why he had come.

"He looked suspicious to me," Dangobert remarked. When Dangobert let him into the *Commissaire*'s presence, Akwa told him bluntly that the visitor must go back.

Coçons needed more reasons to convince him. This, Dangobert offered. The abortive coup, he said was believed to have been foreign-inspired. Ghanaians might have been involved. Ghana had had a long-standing history of unfriendliness with Cameroon. The two countries did not exchange ambassadors.

"This our man could be coming in here to stir up trouble," he said. "He is a potential danger! Besides, the seminar is cancelled."

"Since when did Reverend Akwa know about this cancellation?" the *Commissaire* inquired.

Akwa did not answer. He merely said; "Even if the Seminar were to take place, I would not admit him. He does not possess the right background to attend it."

"I don't understand, Reverend," Coçons said. "You admitted not so long ago that there was a seminar. It was on the strength of your recommendation that we granted him an entry permit to remain in Cameroon for 25 days. Now you are telling us a different story. If, as you say, he is not qualified to attend, then you will have to foot the return ticket. If we ask him to leave before 25 days, that is deportation."

"I admitted him without thoroughly studying the situation. I am sorry. When is the next flight?"

"Tomorrow morning," Dangobert said.

"At what time precisely?"

Dangobert checked and told him: 2 p.m.

Although the *Commissaire* had said nothing concerning any letter bearing his name, Reverend Akwa kept expecting that any minute the latter would be discovered and he would be called up for questioning. The prestige of the church and his personal self, he reflected, cost more, far more than the 50,000 francs he was being asked to pay.

3

Reverend Akwa phoned his house and asked his wife to arrange temporary accommodation for the visitor. He returned later that night, and spent the night wide awake.

Before Reverend Dieudonne Akwa went to bed that night he decided that immediately after breakfast he would ask Akroma to park his things and follow him. He would drive him to the airport and there tell him:

"I have brought you back here so that you return to Ghana. Your coming here is likely to create enormous problems for me personally and for LICE International." He would then hand him over to the airport authorities to send him back to Ghana. But even after that resolve, he had a rough night.

It was his wife who first noticed that there was something the matter with him. She was surprised that he did not snore ten minutes into his sleep, indicating that he did not sleep. Instead she heard him cough and sneeze and sigh. For the first time in years she heard him fanning at mosquitoes. Once or twice she heard him rise and go to the toilet.

When he got up from his insomnia in the morning, however, he felt so uneasy and angry that he thought it wrong to play the nice-host with a **persona non grata.** At breakfast Akroma sat opposite him at the long rectangular table. His wife sat to his left and his daughter Florence sat to his right opposite her mother. Akwa took just one sip of his tea, took a piece of bread in his right hand and then dropped it on his plate again. His wife who had not yet forgotten how little he had slept in the night, watched him for a while and then asked:

"Pastor, anything?"

Reverend Dieudonne Akwa did not answer. He clasped his hands, supported his chin with his thumbs, tightened his lips and said to Akroma who was concentrating on his meal:

"I have to tell you my mind. I am a man of very delicate sensibilities. This your visit has unsettled me terribly. I see embarrassment written all over it. I am a man who does not like to harbour disturbing thoughts. I do not look for them. Ever. What should be disturbing me now is the fate of our church here, the fate of my flock, not that of a questionable and unknown individual. I have had a night like no other in my life. And I do not think I deserve it. There is only one solution to it all. You must have to return back to Accra. There is a flight this afternoon, at 3 p.m. to Accra. You will have to leave. I am sorry about it, but the reputation of this church is at stake. I will write to Reverend Mot Tomlinson to explain why I acted this way."

The bread fell from Akroma's hand into his cup of tea, and he blinked his eyes as though smoke had entered them.

"I am sorry," Reverend Akwa added.

4

Akroma saw all his efforts and careful planning go up in smoke. He knew that Reverend Dieudonne Akwa meant every word he had uttered. He rubbed his right hand across his face and stared with disbelief as though to ensure that it was no dream. His breath became heavy in the instant as though a bag of cement had been placed on his chest. Perspiration burst from all corners of his face. He gnawed at his lip at the same time his eye balls turning redder and redder rolled fiercely out of their sockets and he looked at Reverend Dieudonne Akwa like a tiger staring into the muzzle of a hunter's gun, knowing that there were no two ways, he would have to kill the hunter or be killed. Should he spring on Reverend Dieudonne Akwa, tear him to pieces and jump out and escape? Escape to where? How much of Douala did he know? Besides, he had no chance.

The people would raise an alarm and he would be surrounded immediately and caught, beaten and killed or deported.

As the thought of his utter helplessness took the better of his mind, the ferocity suddenly began to abate until he stared around as if waking from a nightmare. As the animal feeling subsided he began to consider other alternatives. Could he allow himself to be let into the airport building and there hide until the plane had taken off? He recalled the opening under the uncompleted section of the airport through which he could escape. But not knowing the rest of the airport, how far could he go?

Many questions flashed through his mind. But his mind was made up. He would do anything not to return to Ghana. The mere thought of going back to Ghana jangled the very bones of his skull!

"But how can I just go back like that, Reverend?" he pleaded in a trembling voice. "I thought I have tried to explain my problems..."

"Yes. You must go."

Akroma clasped his hands before him and stared on.

"And I have no money," he said almost to himself. Actually he was lamenting the fact that he would have to go back to Ghana without having acquired the money he needed so badly.

"Rev. Akwa is giving me the impression that LICE is an organisation of saints," Akroma said with calculated impudence.

"It may not be," Akwa admitted. "But a normal human being does not advertise his vices the way your missing letter is likely to present us to the world..."

He went into his brief case and drew out an air ticket which he handed over to Akroma. He had already paid for one at the airport, without even asking to know whether Akroma had a return ticket or not.

Akroma took his air ticket with both hands, bowing respectfully but disappointedly.

"I am sorry," Akwa said again, his face stamped in a mask of fury. The personal interest of any single individual cannot be sacrificed for the honour of his organisation, especially in a case like this."

"I understand, Rev, and I thank you very much for your hospitality," Akroma said with disarming humility. Something which made him look like a fool. Perhaps that was the impression he wanted to create. "I was just trying my luck," he said.

"Your luck ran out before you took off," Akwa retorted, sat down, stretched his legs, placed his feet on the central table and picked up his Bible, implying that he had finished with Akroma.

Chapter Nine

(Thursday May 10th 1984)

Essuman Akroma Patrickston was the product of a harsh upbringing which he turned into advantage as he grew up. At the age of seven he had been sent to live with a rather brutal maternal uncle, Boache Danqua, a former head master and a former soldier in the British side during the First World War. As a boy uncle Danqua had harboured hopes of becoming a learned man. When those dreams were shattered by the compulsory conscription, he vowed to transform all of his sister's five children who were placed in his care into the intellectuals he missed becoming.

His favourite policy was simply to compel the children to read whole books or chapters of books and then retell the stories every weekend. The strategy would have worked perfectly because he had many books from which the children would have profited enormously during the years that they lived with him. But things did not go as planned. In the first place, he was married to a lazy woman who never allowed the boys enough time for their reading exercises. Yet, on Saturday nights she was the first to encourage the husband to beat anybody who could not retell the story of a book or summarise a chapter.

In the second place the man always returned home late and drunk, and even on those Saturday evenings he listened to the narratives half-drunk. To save their skin, therefore, the boys would invent titles of non-existent books and summarise non-existent chapters. Thus by the time Akroma and his inmates went to college, and especially long afterwards, he had cultivated the genius of getting himself out of trouble. He could invent the most outrageous lies and get away with them!.

2

Two events marked him out as an evil genius. In 1967 he entered Achimota College, one of the most prestigious institutions in the country. Prior to that year students in the lower and upper sixth were entitled to a monthly allowance of 80 Ghanaian New New Cedis. But the year they went in, following upon the Political upheaval that resulted from the overthrow of President Nkrumah, it was announced that the allowances had been scrapped. Before the announcement was made, however, heads of several institutions had already withdrawn monies to pay the students. As soon as the announcement was made some headmasters decided to pay the students for the last time. Several headmasters chose to use the monies already withdrawn for different purposes. Some, like the headmaster of Achimota decided to put the money into their private accounts.

Akroma could not understand why he would not be given his due. He was particularly pained that his money should be swelling somebody else's bank account. He visited the National Union of Ghanaian Students' Office in Accra and somehow succeeded in securing the official stamp and the stamp pad. He then went into the toilet and stamped some twenty sheets he carried in his small bag. Returning to Achimota he typed the following letter on a stencil which he cut and multiplied, using the stamped sheets.

Dear Headmaster;

A students' uprising is brewing up in your institution and you must take immediate steps to ensure that it does not occur. Students are aware that before the government stopped allowances you had already withdrawn the sum of 12,000 New Cedis which you appear to be trying to use for other purposes than that originally intended.

At this moment the military government will view with much disfavour any actions like these that create further instability in the country. To avert this impending catastrophe, uprising which can end up in untold damages for which your meagre 12,000 New Cedis would be inadequate to compensate, you better pay the monies and remain in the student's good books.

The Principals of twenty colleges in the country who were served the letter of warning paid their students, nobody ever knowing how it came to happen. The president and secretary of the Students Union discovered only afterwards that their stamps had been abused.

3

The second event took place after he had completed from Cape Coast and Legon. While working for G.I.H.O.C (Ghana Industrial Holdings Corporation), forms for the British Council Scholarships were sent to them. Winners of the scholarships were to undergo extensive training in a new area in Remote Sensing called GEOGRAPHIC INFORMATION SYSTEMS AND SATELLITE IMAGE APPLICATIONS.

The boss of the company who had observed Akroma for a very long time wrote a confidential report which would made him lose the scholarship. The report said:

This gentleman is fairly intelligent and obedient, but is mischievous and seems almost incapable of speaking the truth. I disrecommend him for further studies on the GIS-SATIA ticket not because we do not need agric officers, but because I fear such studies will only make him more dangerous to society. Students in this area will be required to handled sensitive and secret material. He cannot be trusted to use his knowledge for good only.

When the Dutch Government sent out forms for people to apply for technical assistance, Akroma simply took the confidential form and filled out:

I give this candidate my highest recommendation. SATIA is exactly what he is best suited for. Careful, dependable and full of initiative, he can be trusted to keep a secret, just what a career such as this prepares him for.

Akroma then forged the Manager's signature and returned to the Dutch embassy. Naturally, he was immediately selected as one of the five Ghanaians to study in GTDNS in Amsterdam. Had the new head of state not repudiated the national debt, and had the Dutch Government not retaliated so harshly, Akroma would have been had no reason to be fighting for survival because he would have been in Holland studying. And this tremendous presence of mind which had always saved him in the past, though somehow dormant, was exactly what he needed at that crucial moment. And it did not abandon him. It rose to the occasion.

4

Akroma's greatest fear was that Akwa might want to take him to the airport himself. Fate worked in his favour. That fear was dispelled when he sat down. He called J-P and instructed him to take Akroma to the airport at 12 noon.

There were two reasons why he did not take Akroma to the airport himself. In the first place he did not want to go there himself because he was sure that the authorities might have seen the tell-tale letter. He would keep clear of the airport until the crook had left the Cameroonian soil. And then, to confound issues, some guests came in just when he was making his last decisions.

Chapter Ten

(Thursday 10th May, 1984)

The weather was typical of late April. The sky was clear and cloudless, the sun hot but tempered by a cold breeze that blew gently, so gently that it was only noticeable by the swaying of the branches and leaves of the mango trees.

At precisely 12 noon, J-P and Akroma left Reverend Akwa's residence. Akroma fingered his air ticket as they drove along. He tapped it on the back of his left hand, his mind running riot. He pulled out his passport, stuck the ticket into it and leaned back, his eyes closed.

As they crossed the Wuri bridge he thought of opening the car and jumping into it and swimming to freedom, of strangling J-P and seizing the vehicle from him. But how much of the town did he know? He would rather work with J-P as far as it was possible.

The journey was doomed to end badly. Mid way into the Wuri Bridge a preposterous taxi-man forced his way out of the long laborious queue and began to overtake the other vehicles . He was virtually driving on the rail lines, (the train passed in the centre of the bridge in a manner which permitted vehicles to pass on either side). As the taxi-man left the queue the other drivers closed up the gap he had created. Then all of a sudden the train appeared. The taxi-man, finding it impossible to rejoin the queue, opened the door and jumped into safely, leaving the train to crush the vehicle with three passengers who were trapped in it. It took a full hour for them to leave the scene and proceed.

Akroma's mind was ticking like a clock. At Rond Point after the bridge Akroma announced:

"I have to go to toilet, please. Stop at the nearest bar."

J-P stopped and looked round.

"How can you go to toilet here? Where?"

"That's a bar," he said. "There must be a toilet there."

Most reluctantly for they might surely miss the plane, J-P pulled up and halted near the Aviation Sportif bar. Akroma got out, taking along with him his passport and air ticket and his brief case. J-P followed him with his eyes, suspiciously.

2

"Let me go to your toilet," Akroma begged the bar man.

"We have only a latrine here, sa. No toilet."

"No problem, I need just somewhere to empty my bowels."

"And to use the latrine, you must have to buy drinks," the bar man said.

Akroma paid for a bottle of Export which he carried with him into the latrine. The latrine had two sections. The first door was marked **VIP's** and the second **General.** The VIP's door was locked. The General was open and had a board which the user could drag and place at the entrance to serve as a door.

In the latrine he did not stoop. He pulled the large board to the door and leaned on his back against it. After ten minutes JP came out of the car and went into the bar to inquire about him. When he came and knocked at the door Akroma answered, made as if he had just eased himself and walked out.

"You think I have escaped?" he joked.

"Ah-ah, how escape, oga?" J-P asked.

Akroma was still holding the opened but undrunk bottle of beer in his hand. They walked to the veranda.

"Sit down, J-P, let me finish my drink."

JP sat down. Akroma took one long drink, swallowed loudly and said in a freezing tone.

"I am in trouble, and I want you to help me."

J-P blinked his eyes copiously and ran his hands over his face.

"I came out here to Cameroon to try my luck and save my family from agony. It looks like I may not, but I am determined to succeed. Only fools suffer, and I am no fool. I have made one mistake with the letter. I cannot afford another mistake."

J-P supported his chin in his right hand, perspiration coursing down his cheek. He seemed to suspect something in the wicked anger that glowed in Akroma's eyes.

"I am not going back to Ghana. I am not continuing from her to anywhere."

In the voice J-P detected a bloodcurdling threat. Akroma seemed to say: "If you do not help me I shall still succeed, and I shall make sure that I kill you before I succeed."

J-P read Akroma's mind well for before he left the latrine Akroma had made up his mind to destroyed anybody who would stand in his way.

3

J-P saw that there was no way he was going to persuade Akroma to get into the car and be driven to the airport. He knew that Akroma was dead serious about what he was saying, although he did not know how the man hoped to carry out his threat. Yet he did not want to be used for such an experiment. It was an obvious risk to let Akroma escape. He might lose his job. But that was a lesser risk than losing his life.

"O-o-ga," he stammered. "You know that they gave you to me to take to the airport…"

"I know, J-P," Akroma said.

"Then even if I want to help you, how shall I talk to Reverend…"

"You took me to the airport and left me there. You were not supposed to carry me into the plane."

J-P reflected for a while. In addition to the threat on his life, he seemed to sympathise with the man's plight. He was even surprised that Akroma had taken the decision to send him back so lightly. He himself had come all the way from Small Monje to seek his fortune in Douala. Had anybody tried to frustrate his plans he would stop at nothing to put such an individual down.

"So I do what, Oga sir? So I can help you how?" he inquired with grave concern.

"First I have said I don't want to leave Cameroon," Akroma said, "but Reverend Pastor Dieudonne Akwa must be made to think that I have left. God has already intervened by not making it necessary for he himself to take me to the airport! Secondly I do not know anybody here. Thirdly, I don't have money. So I need somewhere to hide and plan my survival."

J-P took in a very long breath. What a crushing burden to lay on anybody, he thought.

"I check first," he said and then sat back and pondered for a while. The solution was not long in coming. "I can hide you this night. But after that…."

"That is all I need this minute. Perhaps overnight I will be able to work out some means of escaping into the town. When I succeed in this country, I will never forget that you scarified your life to help me."

J-P drove Akroma to his small apartment in Quartier Deido in the area he called Omnisport. It was an ill-furnished single room with a curtain cutting off the bed area. There were five cane chairs and a small camp bed A kerosene stove stood at the corner to the right as you entered the house. The door to the back let to the general pit latrine from which Akroma could not only hear a woman groan but could hear the excrement drop into the pit. The stench was abominable. Even as they sat Akroma saw two giant rats cross and re-cross the room and disappear under the bed behind the curtain.

"What was that I saw?" Akroma asked.

"My soldiers," J-P joked.

"You cannot kill them?"

"Oga, if you want to kill rats in Douala, the whole town will just begin to smell. Every house has more than twenty. As you are killing, so will they be coming. It looks like the friends are just waiting for you to kill the others so that they come in and take their places."

4

Akroma had a way of making people bend to his will. That same night, whether out of fear for his life or mere naiveté, J-P proved to be of enormous assistance to him. First he told Akroma he would try to convert the air tickets into cash. Although the ideas endeared him to Akroma, it was more because he did not have enough money to feed Akroma than out of good will. He got 50,000francs for each ticket, kept 20,000 francs to himself and told Akroma he lost 20,000 in the deal. Akroma did not object. After all, it was more than he had bargained for. Akroma now had 107,000francs in his purse.

That night too, on his own, while Akroma rested, he went out and after about an hour or so, he announced:

" I have brought you visitors from your country. These are Ghanaians," he said to Akroma. One of them was very tall and dark in complexion with the sort of tribal marks on his jaws which Akroma associated with people from Tamale and the extreme northern part of Ghana. The second was just as dark as the first but slightly shorter and thicker in built. He seemed to carry about him airs of great importance. Akroma could have sworn he was an Ashanti from his looks and accent.

The men shook hands but told J-P in English that he must be making a mistake.

"We are not Ghanaians," one of them, the Ashanti, said in French. "We are from K-Town in the South West Province."

To strengthen their argument, they pulled out Cameroonian identity cards. Akroma eyed them very keenly but said nothing. There was in the eyes of both men the kind of suspicion he associated with Ghanaians. In spite of their I.D. cards, therefore, he insisted that they were Ghanaians who were pretending. Their accent was undoubtedly Ghanaian.

Chapter Eleven

(Friday, May 11th 1984)

Although J-P seemed disappointed at the fact that Akroma had not exploited the acquaintance he had gone so far to create, Akroma went to bed that night having learned something very important: that it was possible for a Ghanaian to obtain a Cameroonian National Identity Card. The following morning, before J-P left for work he told him what he thought.

"I want a Cameroonian I.D. Card."

"How can?" J-P asked , a bit nonplussed.

"Those Ghanaians who claimed to be Cameroonians, did you not see their I.D. cards.?"

"I saw."

"You think if we give a policeman something he will not help you get me one?"

J-P looked at Akroma for some time and then asked:

"Why you need Cameroon I.D.?"

"Very many reasons," Akroma said. "For me to survive I will want to do just anything. There may be things I cannot do if they know that I am not a Cameroonian."

J-P smiled at Akroma's sharpness of mind.

"We try," he said. "We try. But even if the police can help, they will ask for information. You have to sign many things. You have to make fingerprint…"

"If the police agrees to help, they can use even your own finger print. Tell them I am sick in a native doctor's place."

J-P nodded several times and asked:

"Then the names, your parents and…"

"Let me see your own ID," Akroma said.

J-P hesitated. He was beginning so soon to fear Akroma's intelligence.

"Give me your I.D," Akroma repeated.

Unsure and afraid, J-P pulled it out of his pocket and handed it over to him. Akroma studied it for a long time and then said.

"Give any three native names of women in the English-speaking part of Cameroon."

J-P wrote them down for him.

"Give me three male names from the same area,"

Akroma said.

J-P wrote them down.

"Give me the names of villages where you think people with such names could come from."

2

J-P did. What happened next converted Akroma into a genius in J-P's mind. With J-P's I.D. card in front of him., Akroma came up with the following information:

N° SW 24/4227/79
Issued on 17: 7: 79
At: Tiko
Name: Njongo
Surnames: Fabian Mula
Born: 17th June, 1947 . At Likomba
Division: Tiko Sub Division
Province: South West Province
Son of : Oron Njongo Nicolas And Agnes Sendzekof
Occupation: Teaching
Residence: Bonaberi.
Description: Height – 1.89 metres

Special marks – two wounds on left sides of spine; mole on left cheek.

J-P obtained permission from Reverend Akwa to go to the hospital for a check-up. He was therefore able to go to the police station to find out about his friend's problem. He told the police man the man for whom he needed the service was sick and needed to travel. When he promised to give the policeman 5,000francs, the man believed everything else and, had he brought a passport picture with him he would have returned with the card that same afternoon.

When he reached home he told Akroma it would cost him 10,000francs. He had thus made 5,000 francs from the deal. A passport picture was taken that night . J-P returned from work the following day with a Cameroonian I.D. card for Akroma.

Chapter Twelve

(Saturday May 12th, 1984)

In the night, as soon as the I.D. Card entered his hands, Akroma said it would be unsafe for him to continue to be in J-P's house. He said he would need to transfer to a more obscure place.

"We Ghanaians, we don't trust each other. Those my Ghanaian brothers you brought may betray me," he told J-P. If they could declare in his presence that they were not Ghanaians, he thought, then they would not hesitate to betray anybody whom they did not trust. "I have the feeling," he said, "that they sensed I knew they were lying that they were Cameroonians."

2

J-P closed from work at 12 noon. The two men then sat down and tried to find ways by which Akroma could make some money.

"You have worry eyes," J-P told him at one point. "You can do kind kind things."

Akroma shrugged. J-P continued.

"You can form a church like I have seen people doing. I go to Kumba with my friends and say we are blind. We beg for one or two months. Or we say we are lame. You announce your church and they say you can make the blind to see the lame walk. We ask people to lead us to you, and you make us see and walk. See? Is that not how Reverend Akwa brought his church here?"

Akroma smiled.

"That's kind of you, J-P," he said, "But I only want to hide, not expose my identity. I cannot indulge in any activity at this moment that is likely to draw too much attention to myself and make people want to know me. Not so soon."

"We must have to think about it,: J-P told him.

"I need another I.D. Card,: Akroma said.

"Why ?" J-P asked.

"Well, I just need it," Akroma said. "If at any time in the future I would like to be called by any other name, I would like to be ready to do that."

J-P looked at Akroma's intelligence with awe. There seemed to be no end to his creativity. But he said it would be difficult to go to the police and apply for another card. That, he argued, would drag them both into trouble.

After a few minutes' reflection Akroma asked whether there were any places in town where people left their I.D. cards at the entrance before going in.

"Radio Station, SONEL and in the embassies," J-P told him.

Akroma suggested that J-P should lead him to one of such places, preferably the Radio Station. On Monday, after work Akroma and J-P took a taxi to the Douala Radio Station. Akroma studied the way people went in and out, drew j-P aside and told him:

"It is as I expected. You see that the guards are just playing their cards. They are not taking any particular notice of who is taking what. We put our cards there, go in and when we are going out we take our cards along with two others, you take one I take one."

It worked exactly as Akroma thought, except for the fact that the Card J-P took turned out to belong to a lady. The card Akroma picked up belong to a certain **Bidias Polycarp Abessolo**, born in Bokito in Mbam Division in 1939.

Chapter Thirteen

(Tuesday May 15th 1984)

On Tuesday night Akroma moved to Hotel de Quartre Boutons in the Logbaba area called Swine Quarter, right in the heart of Ndokoti. It was not a hotel that could be described by its stars partly because of its location and partly because of its size and amenities.

There were no more than 15 rooms in all. Only four of the rooms were self-contained and these were located on the upper floor. The rest of the rooms shared toilets – two rooms to a toilet. The toilets themselves were very old and broken. The sinks had no covers and users needed to pull a string or wire to cause them to flush. The curtains, even in the upper rooms were threadbare. In some of the rooms the louvers had long been broken and were now replaced with pieces of plywood.

It was a very cheap hotel frequented mainly by pimps and prostitutes and men who brought women and girls to have a "Rest".

They charged him 3000 francs for the night. Akroma took a room on the ground floor from which he could see any vehicles or anybody coming into or leaving the hotel. He did not want to be surprised by any policeman.

As soon as he moved in he started working out the plan of action. He told them he would be there for a week. The name he gave was the one of the I.D Card they had just established. During that time he was sure to find a free woman, fall in love with her and move in to live with her. If he succeeded and was able to give the woman 1000 francs each morning for the market, he could save a lot while looking for ways to make money.

To conceal his identity he bought a hung Afro-Wig meant for women and had it trimmed to such an extent that it reached down just above his eyebrows. This made it difficult for anybody who had known him casually before to recognise him. He also bought a pair of dark sun glasses which he wore even in the dark. To accentuate this disguise he also decided (since he was naturally a very hairy man), to grow a thick moustache and a beard. He also decided to become a stammerer. That would explain why he would not readily join in any conversation wherever he went.

2

As part of his strategy, Akroma took four more passport photos at DAWNMAN GOLDEN PHOTOS just adjacent to the hotel. In the secrecy of the hotel he replaced the picture on each of the two .I.D. Cards with his own and kept both cards, He did not know why he needed the two extra cards, but instinctively, he decided to keep them, should a situation arise. He had planned to take the negative. But by the rarest of oversight he forgot to do so, and this would cost him very much inconvenience .

Almost directly opposite Quartre Boutons, was a small bar called NOSTROMO. When he first checked into the hotel it was called DRIVERS' CLUB, and the latter board still stood near the back door. It was run by a gentleman whom everybody addressed as Ngia. He was a hulky two metres in height, smoked endlessly, and seemed to be revered by every guest who came there. Akroma would leave the hotel, stroll to the road and then come there as though he was coming from somewhere else.

Ngia was at home with French, English and Spanish. He looked enormously strong and had the hands of a strangler. He could hold a jug of palm wine in just one hand, and at the base. Seasoned sportsmen among his customers called him Yashin, after the Russian goalkeeper who was said to be capable of holding a football in his palm as though it was a tennis ball.

Whoever Yashin was, Ngia was not much different because he could serve the palm wine from a four-litre jug, holding it at the base as though it was a regular bottle.

He was always ready to attend to his customers. He had infinite patience, and Akroma came to this conclusion when he saw how Ngia listened to a certain semi-lunatic of a woman who came there very often. She would be driven out of every other bar, but as soon as she got to NOSTROMO she felt so much at ease that she was even able to tell people the source of her madness: a curse from members of a family into which she was supposed to get married. Ngia would listen, encourage her, and in addition, would give her a draught of the palm wine while refusing to give the same quantity out to more worthy customers.

Akroma took an interest in the place because each time he looked out of his window he would see cars parked in front of the ramshackle place. He would hear District Officers, University lecturers, poets and police Commissaries discuss politics, football and other trivialities. All these important personalities, he learned later, were classmates and childhood friends of the enigmatic Ngia.

NOSTROMO sold not only beer and palm wine but also illicit gin and cooked foods. Akroma visited the place for the first time one evening in the company of J-P. He never actually introduced himself to anybody in the place. They all called him "Oga sa," the way J-P did each time they were together. They were all very entertaining and friendly people. The leader and motivating force of the daily entertainment was somebody they all called "Green Snake" He told one joke after the other on any known subject and the whole place was alive each time he was sighted from the distance.

On his second visit to the bar he saw two women walk past them. As he did not speak French he jokingly asked Ngia to call them for him They came as if they were expecting to be invited. Akroma offered the two women a single drink, they took 33 Export. As they drank and conversed he seemed to like the elderly lady who introduced herself as Severina, and her sister as Felicitas. She was of moderate height and very dark in complexion. She spoke softly and seemed to avoid looking him in the face. She had rather wide expressive eyes which she held down for most of the time. Her lips were thick and she had a small gap in the upper row of her teeth.

The other lady, Felicitas, was younger but Akroma did not like her. She was light in complexion in a manner which suggested that she had changed the colour of her skin. She talked fast and carelessly and seemed to be arrogant. She was a high school student and spoke as if the high school was a university, as if nobody around her had ever been to school.

After their drink Akroma invited Severina to his hotel. She did not object, and while there Akroma discovered a friend. She was a seamstress who generally lived alone expect during vacations when her juniors sisters came to spend some time with her. She was a good friend because Akroma found her very gullible. She believed every word of it when Akroma told her that he was an oil Merchant from Liberia who was looking for sources of investment; his money had been seized at the airport by the customs and police, but he was determined not to give up. He had already sent a message back to Liberia to request for more money to begin his research.

4

Schools were to reopen in about a week and as soon as Felicitas returned to school Akroma could come to live with her instead of spending so much money on hotel bills. He gave his name as Kojo Thompson Abreba.

Severina brought him food in the evenings and spent the night with him. On other occasions she would invite him to dine with them, Akroma footing the bills. On the fourth day she brought Akroma a small kerosene stove with which he used to prepare minor dishes for himself.

Chapter Fourteen

(Friday 18th May, 1984)

On Wednesday the following week, eleven days after Akroma as supposed to have left Cameroon Reverend Dieudonne Akwa was invited for questioning by the *Commissaire* at the Airport.

"A cleaner discovered this letter under the wash-hand sink in the toilet."

Reverend Dieudonne Akwa opened the letter and read:

Dear Rev. Akwa;

May God bless you. We received the news from Cameroon about the political upheavals with a lot of shock and consternation. May the Lord be praised that all has virtually come to pass.

Let me, brother-in-Christ, step a little bit out of the beaten path of religion to suggest something that would have sounded odious under different circumstances, and which I would never have dared to mention if I did not know that you would be of help. The bearer of this message is the son of Akromahene, the Ghanaian Chieftain whose generosity and kind understanding made it possible for LICE to settle here in the Greater Accra Region of Ghana to the extent that we have done. The family has presented us here with a problem which we have to solve to salvage our good name here. He will tell you what problems he has. You do not need to try to solve them. You only need to cooperate with him.

I am aware of the indefinite postponement of the Episcopal Seminar formerly slated for May 14th. But we are using the Seminar as an excuse to let him into Cameroon. This letter is mainly to introduce him to you and to inform you that he has our blessing in whatever else he wants to do in Cameroon. Once in he will be able to fend for himself He has promised me to be of good behaviour! Cameroons is a land of endless opportunities. Let us give him a chance, in God's name.

2

It was the letter which Reverend Mot Tomlinson had given Akroma, and which he had lost at the airport.

"I must congratulate you for your foresight," the *Commissaire* told Reverend Dieudonne Akwa.

"I am glad you saw with me, *Monsieur Le Commissaire,* and sent him away. I suspected that there was something the matter with him. Thank God we set him back."

The matter ended there, at least for a while. On Monday the 21st of May Reverend Akwa was again invited to the airport. Inspector Dangobert had made further investigations on the Akroma issue and had come to a conclusion which he handed over to his boss.

"Reverend Akwa," the *Commissaire* began, "that your Akroma did not leave Douala for Accra. Nobody bearing his name left for Ghana."

"What does this mean, *Monsieur Le Commissaire*?" Reverend Akwa inquired worriedly.

"It means that he is certainly still in Cameroon," the *Commissaire* said.

Reverend Dieudonne Akwa's smooth face creased into a haggard frown. He pulled down the sides of his mouth, pulled out a handkerchief and mopped perspiration that broke instantly on his face.

"This Akroma problem is eating me like a canker worm," he said, "and how I wish it should end. To my mind, *Monsieur Le Commissaire*, that man left. My driver is still out there, who took him to the airport, *Monsieur Le Commissaire.*"

Reverend Akwa immediately sent for J-P.

J-P defended himself as best he could. He had driven the visitor to the entrance into the lounge and had waited until the plane had taken off with the passengers. Because he did not suspect anything, he had not stayed back to actually ensure that Akroma had effectively gone away.

Reverend Dieudonne Akwa stared into J-P's face like a cobra and warned him: "If that man is still in this country, and if it is discovered that you had your hand in this matter, you will pay dearly for it."

"But how can I do such a thing, Reverend?" J-P queried.

Reverend Akwa merely shrugged his shoulders.

"We will get in touch with you again," the *Commissaire* told Reverend Dieudonne Akwa dismissively. "Be on the lookout."

Chapter Fifteen

(Sunday , May 20th 1984)

The following day Dangobert went up to *Commissaire* Blanche Diamant, the *Commissaire* for Tightened Security. This was the branch of the security system specially designed to protect the Head of State. It was this department that uncovered plots against the Head of State. Diamant, a white man from Bordeaux in France, earned a salary of eight million francs per month for doing just that – smelling plots and crushing them in the buds, or inventing them where they were slow in coming. It was widely believed that though the 6th April coup had taken them all by surprise, it was Coçons' timely intervention that helped foil it.

He was about sixty with hair that grew thickly on his head, descending to just above his heavily lined forehead. He had a very long aquiline nose over his small and withdrawn mouth giving the impression that he had lost many of his front teeth. He wore a pair of old-fashioned goggles behind which glittered a pair of sharp blue eyes. Nobody knew how he got to be where he was because very few people associated him with much intelligence. Although he always insisted that all matters of security be referred to him first, he had never been known to make a suggestion that had not been countered by even the newest recruits. But he seemed to command a lot of respect from the powers above.

2

When Dangobert took the Akroma file up to Diamant, the *Commissaire* told him confidently: "It is easy to tell that such a man is in Cameroon, you just leave it in my hands." He knew that his was a most delicate job and did not think a black man was capable of suggesting anything to him. He hated taking advice, especially from a black man. Dangobert seemed to him far too meddlesome. He belonged to the Emi-Immigration, and not Tightened Internal Security.

The very next day *Commissaire* Blanche Diamant made the vital move to track down Akroma. An announcement was made over the radio and television, inviting all foreigners, especially Ghanaians to report to the department of Internal Security with their resident permits and/or passports. At the end of the exercise *Commissaire* Diamant concluded:

"That man left. All foreigners have been checked. He is not amongst them."

Dangobert felt disappointed.

"Does the *Commissaire* think that if that man was in Cameroon, he would go and give himself up to the authorities?"

Diamant did not answer.

"So what do you want to see done?' he asked at last.

"We have to track him down."

"We who? I am here to uncover treason, to protect the head of state, not to track down mosquitoes. If you think you will do it, go right ahead."

This gave Inspector Dangobert the license to pursue the Akroma fugitive.

3

On returning from work on the Monday that Reverend Akwa was invited to be told that Akroma did not leave Cameroon, J-P went straight to Akroma's hotel and warned:

"Oga, trouble is coming. You must hide more more. They saw a letter you lost at the airport. They phoned Ghana. They now know that you did not go back. If they see you they shall kill me. So hide well well."

Akroma did not look as shocked as J-P had expected. He simply exhaled a very long breath, scratched his head several times, bit his lips and said calmly:

"I will surely hide." It was as though he had expected that all along. He, however, decided to cut down his daily movements. He then invited Severina to spend the next week with him. He had his vital belongings packed into a small brief case which he carried each time he left the hotel. These included a pair of underpants, a pair of socks, a singlette, two shirts and a small envelope containing his passport and I.D. cards. He did not care about anything else that he left behind him.

Chapter Sixteen

(Wednesday May 23rd 1984)

He did well to hide. But he was not to hide forever. On Wednesday, two days before he was to pack out of the hotel Akroma left to go for a stroll. He went out occasionally to continue to understand the town and study various means of making money.

Severina did not lock the door behind him as she usually did each time he left. Akroma had bought a bottle of gas which he left half open and concealed under the bed. She lit the kerosene stove and put some water on it to make *garri*. While the water was warming up she lit a cigarette, poured herself a full glass of illicit gin and began to drink and smoke. She felt a bit tipsy and sat on the bed. She then lay down and closed her eyes, unconscious of the gas that was slowly issuing from the bottle and moving towards the cigarette and the stove.

2

It was Ngia who first noticed that a thin column of smoke was issuing from the window of Akroma's room. As the smoke increased he immediately raised an alarm and people rushed in to see what was going on. All of a sudden the curtains caught fire and with that, the entire room was ablaze. The hotel had no fire extinguishers and, buckets of water which were hauled into the flames merely intensified the conflagration. When his door was broken into and the fire finally put out, it was not possible to tell whether the charred remains of the occupant were those of a man or a woman.

By a sheer coincidence, an ubiquitous Dangobert was returning to work after break when he saw fumes from a distance and heard people shouting all over the place. The causes of the fire as well as the extent of the damage were still being speculated when he arrived the scene.

"Any loss of lives?" Dangobert inquired.

"Yes," a lady said. She was one of Severina's friends.

"Our Moyo was inside. A certain man like that," she said. "He used to come and visit my sister." She ran to DAWNMAN GOLDEN PHOTOS and pulled out one of the passport pictures Akroma had taken, and which the photographer had pinned on a board for the purpose of advertisement.

While Dangobert was still studying the picture, Felicitas, Severina's sister who had also just arrived the scene, pointing in J-P's direction and said:

"Aha, that is Moyo's friend, that man who used to come and visit him."

J-P fled from the scene, but not before Dangobert had caught a glimpse of him. About 200 metres from the hotel stood the Credit Union Building, a gigantic five storey structure near which Severina worked as a seamstress. About 500 metres from the Credit Union Building stood the Congress Hall in which all Government celebrations took place. As J-P was shuffling his way through the crowded street he sighted Akroma standing under Casino Royal, a discarded hotel that stood opposite the Congress Hall.

He struggled and got to Akroma just as he too was leaving to go down towards his hotel, perhaps to see if his diabolic plan had worked.

"God bless you, Oga," J-P said, placing his hand on his chest.

"Why?" Akroma asked.

"Quarter Bouton is on fire. The fire started with your section and burned all the people inside. They are saying you are inside. Thank God."

Akroma smiled dryly and shook his head.

"As you can see," he said, "I was not inside. But I left my Severina resting. Did they see her?"

J-P shook his head in denial and added.: "I say nobody inside escaped."

Akroma turned and made as if he was going towards the hotel.

"You try, you die," J-P said.

Akroma stood back and looked at J-P in mock consternation.

"Yes," J-P said. "I ran away because I saw Felicitas standing with that Inspector Dangobert. They were all looking at one of your passport pictures which DAWNMAN GOLDEN PHOTOS had put on the board."

"My picture?"

"Yes"

"How did it get there?"

"When you take a picture the photographer leave one there to advertise. Felicitas was holding it."

"Did Dangobert see you?"

"If he did not see me, why should I be fearing? When they pointed me I escaped me."

Akroma took in a long breath. He seemed more touched by the news of his picture and Dangobert's presence than by the death of Severina.

"Let us go back across the street into Old Town and sit down and think," he suggested. "We have a problem now."

Chapter Seventeen

Akroma had visited almost all the corners of Deido. When he suggested New City Hotel in Old Town, he knew why. They crossed the Commercial Avenue, passed through Waterside bar and climbed into New City. There they sat in the Off License section from which they could watch people pass without anybody seeing them. When they were seated Akroma spoke first. He said: "J-P, we have a problem. And we have to solve it. Thank God I travel like a snail, with all my things in this bag. If my bag was inside there I would be a dead man."

"We have to escape," J-P said.

"Me or we?" Akroma asked.

"I have told you that Dangobert saw me. He now knows that we have been together. I know that he will be looking for me. They will arrest me. I think Oga does not know that what I have done can kill me."

"I know," Akroma said, with a touch of remorse. After a moment's reflection he said: "My worry is, where are we escaping to?"

"The place that comes to my head is Yaounde. I get many many friends there."

"Is it like Douala?" Akroma asked.

"Like Douala how?"

"Many people, many things happening? This Douala is like Accra. You can even hide an elephant in your house and your neighbour will not know. People are too busy doing their own things to look into what you do or what you are…"

"Douala and Yaounde, no difference. Only that places are scattered. Except in Briketeri where people live like here, no difference. We go and see. If things are not good, we run away."

"What of your house and the things. What of your job?"

"No worry, Oga, na man di loss. For my things, no problem. You saw them yourself. Are those things?" Bamboo chairs, latrine in the parlour? I can leave them there. I owe rents for one year. If they sell those things thy will not be up to what I owe. I only want to escape with my head. In the night I will go and gather my clothes and we escape in the morning."

"What of your job?"

"What I am doing, is that work? Every morning, 'Good morning Pastor' and at the end of the month they give you 15,000frs. If I had something better to do will I call that work?"

2

The fire disaster occurred on Wednesday afternoon. On Thursday, May 24th, the day when Akroma would have been moving in to live with Severina, the two men boarded a bus for Yaounde. As the *travelling* regulations demanded, they handed their I.D cards to the park collector who took down their names in what they called the Bordereau. J-P gave his I.D. card, while Akroma gave the one he had stolen from the Radio Station but which now bore his picture. The name on the card was Bidias Polycarp Abessolo

Barely 15 kilometres from Douala they ran into a road-block. The traffic police had barred their way and was checking among other things, tax tickets. This was something Akroma had not foreseen. In Ghana there were no such checks! Akroma and a few others were asked to descend from the vehicle because they did not possess the tickets. When he noticed that the other delinquents were giving bribes of 1000frs and being allowed to climb back into the vehicles, he did same.

Although he easily bribed his way through the police checkpoint, Akroma remained extremely uneasy. So uneasy did he feel that at Esseka, about 100 kilometres from Douala he told J-P who was sitting by his side:

"When we are escaping like this, we should not travel straight. Something in me tells me that somebody may be following us. Suppose we get to another checkpoint and they wanted to know more about me? We could even be travelling in the same vehicle with the man whose ID. Card I took."

"So what are you saying that we do?"

"We get off at the end of the town," he said.

"And sit down and plan again," Akroma said.

At Odenepouk, a small village just at the outskirts of Esseka, Akroma informed the driver of the bus that they had forgotten the file because of which they were going to Yaounde. They had therefore to go down.

"If you go down you will not get back your money," the driver told them.

"No palaver," Akroma said. They climbed down. They walked across the street and went to sit down behind a roadside bar.

"So what do we do now?" J-P inquired

"We think of what to do. Yaounde is the obvious place where they will think we have gone, if they are looking for us."

3

They lingered by the road side for a while until the bus drove off. They then crossed the road went into the back room of an off-licence bar and sat down.

"Where are we?" Akroma inquired

J-P told him.

"Why?" he asked.

"I don't know," Akroma said, "but my blood tells me that we should not go any further. We do not have to go back to Douala. We can even remain here…"

"Here?" J-P asked. "But this will be the first place to look for us when they hear that we left the bus here."

Akroma ordered a cold *33 Export* while J-P took a *Jobajo* for himself. After emptying a glass J-P walked out, stood at the veranda for about ten minutes and then returned with an EUREKA.

"I have thought of something," he told Akroma. Akroma looked at him and asked softly: "So what have you thought of J-P?"

"You see, Oga sa, when you have a problem and you think, there is always an answer. It is like if God made us to stop here…"

Akroma stared at him with growing interest.

"I am listening," he said.

J-P led him out and they walked across the street to the other side . There J-P pointed to an untarred road..

"Is this not the road to Nijombari," he asked.

"Who is Nijombari?" Akroma asked.

"Is a place, not a person,"

"I see. So how does that help us?"

"Is it not where Pa Sabbas lives?"

"Who is Pa Sabbas?"

"Is he not the same womb with my mother?"

Akroma smiled faintly.

"Did I not live with him for a long time?" J-P asked.

"What does he do there?"

"Business. He works there. He used to have money, plenty. We go and hide there. Nobody will think we are there."

Akroma nodded with great satisfaction.

"That's the kind of place I want," he said. "How far from here?"

"Only that the road is bad. It is only about 70 kilometres. But it will take many hours."

J-P had one worry: "But who am I going to say that you are, oga, since we are escaping?"

Akroma had worked that out in his mind.

"No problem," he told J-P. "I am an investor from Liberia. I have not had time to tell you that I ran and operated a mineral extraction firm in Koforidua in Ghana. I will tell anybody I am a mineral investor from Liberia. Any Cameroonian should be glad to meet a foreign mineral investor and do business with him.

"I'll say I am here to try to exploit the gold and bauxite in the west coast of Cameroon. You will say you have abandoned your job to help show me around on this very profitable venture. Let's try and see what this fetches us. The rest of it I shall be able to handle."

It was concluded.

Chapter Eighteen

(Tuesday May 29th 1984)

On Monday Dangobert invited Felicitas (who claimed that the burnt Akroma was her sister's lover) to his office. Her sister had not turned up, she told him, and there was still no sign of her anywhere.

"I have two guesses," Dangobert told her. "the first is that your sister and that her Akroma husband could have been both in that room when it caught fire."

Felicitas sobbed, carried her hands on her head and screamed so loudly that people rushed in from the other offices. Dangobert managed to calm her down.

"It is only a guess, young lady;" Dangobert tried to soothe her.

"Yes sir, but it makes me fear because since it happened I have not seen my sister and I have not seen that her boy friend. What was the second guess, sir?'

Dangobert wanted to say it was also possible that it was Felicitas' sister alone who got burnt in the hotel, and that Akroma could very well have set fire on the hotel to distract his pursuers. But he saw that the guess would just break Felicitas's heart. Instead he said:

"My second guess is that it could be Akroma who got burnt and that when it happened your sister fled for fear of being accused of setting the hotel on fire."

Felicitas looked at Dangobert for a very long time, cleaned her eyes but said nothing. All efforts to trace her sister had failed. J-P did not report for work on Monday. That evening

Dangobert went to J-P's house where he learned that he had not been seen since Sunday evening. By midnight he had established that it was more likely than not that the charred body in the hotel was that of Severina, and not Akroma. Akroma must, therefore, be on the run.

2

On Wednesday morning he went to the bus stations and checked from the duplicate copy of the *bordereau* of passengers who had travelled out of Douala since Monday to the South West, North West or Central Provinces, J-P's name was in the *bordereau* of a vehicle bound for Yaounde that left that morning. In fact, it had just left.

Dangobert telephoned his office to request for a vehicle to chase the fugitives. He took his service car and drove at break-neck speed, overtaking every bus to Yaounde. When he arrived Poma, he thought he should check before proceeding. To his greatest relief, the first bus had not reached there.

One hour thirty minutes later the first bus arrived. He stopped it, climbed in excitedly and conducted a quick check. Two passengers had gotten off the bus at Doroke and had returned to Douala because, as they said, they had left an important document. One of the persons was Jean-Paul Mobangui. The other was Polycarp Abesolo. Akroma, he concluded, must be travelling now under a false name.

Dangobert had thus wasted his trip. He returned to Douala disappointed but determined more than ever to get equal with the culprits.

Part Two

Chapter Nineteen

(Wednesday, May 23rd 1984)

The journey to Nijombari was disturbing to both Akroma and J-P in several respects. For J-P, he was unsure of what to tell his uncle in whose hands he grew, and whom he had abandoned for some six years, without sending a word of greetings back to them. He was not coming back to pass but to stay. And he was not coming alone. He was coming with a stranger who had made of him a criminal or an accomplice on the run. He wondered how he would be received.

Akroma was far more comfortable. It was a leap in the dark he had taken, but he was sure he would make it. Existence for him now had become a fate that simply had to be outsmarted, no matter the circumstances, no matter the complication or degree of uncertainty surrounding it. He had one paramount consolation: he was on his way to somewhere, from one town in Cameron to another, or nowhere. But that was not as bad being on the plane back to Ghana as Reverend Dieudonne Akwa would have loved to see.

2

The trip from Edea to Nijombari took three hours. The road, if it could be called that, was an untarred track made worse by heavy timber trucks that plied it all the year round. On that fateful day it began to rain very heavily as soon as they drove away. Here and there were buses, land rovers, trucks and private cars stuck in pools of water and mud in the middle or by the side of the road, with mechanics bending over or lying under to try to get the vehicles moving again. Here and there motor owners, drivers and passengers stood or sat gloomily silent or conversed sadly about the fate of their vehicles, how Belgium was flooding Cameroon with rotten vehicles and swindling huge sums of monies from ignorant buyers, how they had been tricked into boarding an old vehicle, how a dealer had sold them the wrong parts, or how mechanics had taken monies and had failed to take care of the repairs. Ironically, the roads were worse as you approached the villages, and it was alleged that this was because villagers deliberately dug gutters across the roads to create problems for drivers whom they then stood by to help drivers out for a fee whenever the situation arose.

At every stop there were little girls and boys hawking groundnuts, bananas, pears, coconuts, kola-nuts, oranges, pine apples and the like. On one occasion Akroma tried to put his wits to the test. He chose for this experiment an innocent little girl who had showed a tray of groundnuts into the bus. He grabbed a handful and when she screamed he quickly transferred a good quantity to his left hand and threw back just a few grains. The little girl walked away without noticing how much she had had lost. It was when Akroma noticed that an elderly passenger had seen him that he smiled and called for the little girl to whom he gave back some of the ground nuts.

"Stupid girl," Akroma said. "Can't sell things well." He smiled to the old man who was forced to smile back.

3

There were farmlands on both sides of the road, interspersed with palm and rubber plantations and on which people of all ages were at work. Akroma remembered a trip to Tamale in Northern Ghana which he had once undertaken to do his Teaching Practice, while he was still in the University of Cape Coast. That trip was made through an extremely bad road they called Kintampo. Nothing that he saw in the Nijombari road, though, came close to his experience along the Kintampo stretch.

Declaring that he was a visitor from Likomba in the Southern West Province, he said he was coming in search of his junior sister who eloped with a driver some seven years ago into Nijombari, leaving behind her in his care a daughter of only a year old.

He got the intended response: everybody sympathised with him and was ready to tell him as much as he wanted to know about the place. It was a town of about 150,000 inhabitants. Administratively it was a Sub-District. Health wise, it had two Government Hospitals and four dispensaries located at various corners in the town. There were no less than three pharmacies and a host of patent medicine stores. As far as education was concerned, there were three Grammar Schools – a *general* Lycee, a Lycee Technique, and a Lycee Bilingue. There were about ten private colleges and an uncountable number of Evening Schools.

In sports, Nijombari had once boasted of a team that played in the first division for five years. For the last four years, however, the best team in the district had not gone beyond the semi-finals of the Second Division tournaments.

In the area of business which interested Akroma the most, he was glad to hear, as J-P had said of Douala, that anybody of talent could always enjoy his life there. Apart from the regular business of supermarkets, there were rich traders who bought and sold coffee, cocoa and palm produce. A big market also existed in the mining industry. The mining industry was owned and run by extremely rich investors, many of whom made their fortunes by smuggling bauxite and diamonds.

4

Nijombari city itself was untarred, although it had street lights and a telephone system. NO SWEAT, NO SWEET, the bus that brought them from Esseka dropped them at *the Stationement Central* whence they were to look for a taxi to Quarter Nobem where J-P's uncle lived

"I still wonder how I will introduce you to my uncle,"

J-P said as soon as they had taken down their bags.

Akroma took out a piece of paper on which he wrote the details which J-P would need.:

Name: Mr. Kojo Hanson

Occupation: Investor from Liberia who has come to investigate and set up investment possibilities. He is travelling incognito because he wants to avoid taxes from the Government.

Once that introduction was done, he, Akroma, would take care of the rest.

J-P shook his head in endless dismay.

"Then why am I *travelling* with you, if my uncle wants to know?" J-P asked.

"You will tell them that you were so attracted by the kind of business I want to set up," Akroma said, "that you resigned your job with the LICE to follow me."

Chapter Twenty

(Wednesday, May 23rd 1984)

It took Akroma and J-P twenty minutes to find a taxi that would take them right to Nobem where J-P's uncle lived. The taxi branched off the main road and then drove up a slippery but apparently much-used track that led to a half-broken gate.

"Uncle Sabas lives here," J-P announced. They paid the taximan, J-P lifted his valise and Akroma with his brief case in his right hand followed him up to the gate. There J-P stopped as if he was trying to recall some important detail. Because of the cypress trees that grew dottedly outside the cement blocks gate they were out of view of anybody standing in the veranda of the house.

"You have forgotten what to tell him about me?" Akroma asked.

"How can I forget," P-P asked. But Akroma noticed that there was some uncertainty in his voice. He advised J-P to repeat the information. He started by saying: "Oga here is Mr. Akroma from Liberia…"

Akroma corrected him and then they entered the compound. It was half past five and dusk was not far off.

2

J-P entered the compound voice first.

"Is pa in?" he called aloud.

"Why don't we go in quietly?" Akroma asked.

"Pa has many many dogs…" J-P began when somebody rose to the veranda and inquired in an equally loud voice:

"Who is talking there like my son Mombangui?"

"I am the one, pa. Where are the dogs?"

The man smiled to himself and said:

"I cannot even feed myself, you are talking of dogs? Come you in."

The man waited on the first step of the veranda until they reached him. He tried to take J-P's bag.

"No, pa, I can carry it."

J-P was no stranger to the house. He walked ahead of his uncle into the parlour.

"Where is mammy Anna?" he inquired excitedly.

"Inside," the man said.

J-P put his bag and that of Akroma in the parlour and then went to the veranda behind the house and greeted his uncle's wife.

Akroma took one look at the man and concluded at once that he was a man he could use. He looked like somebody who had once tasted wealth. He could have passed for a man of eighty, but he must have been just about sixty years old and there was every evidence that although he looked thin he had once carried a large belly. He had a longish head with brown hair, evidence of continuous but unsuccessful use of dyes to keep the colour black.

He was slightly bald, with a flat forehead, a flat nose and a large mouth that reddened at the corners when he smiled. He wore his large khaki pair of trousers well over his navel which he held in place with a belt so old that it looked like a rope. His eyes darted suspiciously and there was a certain nervousness about him which Akroma could not explain. There was one obvious characteristic about his face: he did not look intelligent.

The woman, probably in her late fifties, received the visitors with undisguised as well as unexplained displeasure. J-P felt particularly embarrassed. He remembered how very friendly the woman was when he was living with them some ten years ago. She would go down the road to receive visitors she had never met before, show them where to sit and offer them something to eat or drink while they waited for her husband.

That was long ago when contractors and college proprietors were the hottest cakes in town, the only cocks to crow. The visitors would learn later that as soon as Pa Sabbas's fortunes took a downward plunge, his relationship with his wife as well as her relationship with his friends and relatives took a different turn. Akroma had never met her before. Her reception caused him bitter pangs because it immediately warned him that to live with them he must work extremely hard and fast to win her to their side.

People who used to visit them and spend weeks with them suddenly became debt collectors, ready to compel Pa Sabbas to sell his property to pay them. People who strolled into the compound as if on a harmless casual visit ended up dragging her husband to the police. And because Pa Sabbas never disclosed the extent of his indebtedness to his wife, she suddenly developed an aggressive attitude towards her husband and all his friends. She had come to develop a profound suspicion of the motives of anybody visiting them.

Her aggression took very many forms. She never saw eye-to-eye with her husband. In all arguments in which he was involved, it was always her husband's point of view that was wrong. Nothing that her husband did impressed her,, even when everybody thought differently. For instance, once when he returned from town having had a hair-cut, everybody noticed and praised it. One woman actually said he looked several years younger and asked him to tell her husband where it was done so that he too could look handsome, When his wife was forced to notice it two days afterwards she asked him whether the barber was blind.

"Even me I can barb better than such a thing that he has carved on your head," she ended up.

Pa Sabbas was used to it and so her absurd conduct never surprise him.

Chapter Twenty-One

(Wednesday, May 23rd,1 984)

The three men returned to the veranda. There, J-P introduced his companion as "Kojo Hanson, a Liberian businessman in quest of investment opportunities." As he noticed the excitement with which Pa Sabbas received the news, he ended by saying "If an opportunity like this comes my way in Douala and I know I can bring him here, why should I, your own child, allow somebody else gain from it?"

Pa Sabbas looked 80, but was about 60, having been victim of some of the worst trials, Akroma would learn later. A sudden overwhelming exhilaration ran through charged through the old man's blood like an electric current. This bit of information caused Pa Sabbas to rise from his arm chair and greet him with very special reverence. It also caused his wife to come to the door to take a closer look at the businessman. Pa Sabbas asked them what they would take and immediately sent for the drinks.

While the drinks were being brought Pa Sabbas asked to know more about J-P's friend. It was Akroma himself who explained:

"I am a bauxite merchant. I have business in Ghana and Liberia and I have come out here to expand. I need somebody with land which I can buy and set up my industries. But I am *travelling* incognito. I don't want my presence known until I shall have made all my feasibility studies."

J-P was not only amazed by what he was hearing but also by the cocksure attitude with which Akroma was talking. He began to doubt whether he had ever really known the man he was travelling with. He certainly doubted Akroma's claims, but simply looked on since his entire future depended on how his listeners would respond to what he would say.

"Do you have land, or know anybody who has land?" Akroma asked Sabbas.

"About how large, sir?" the man inquired with keenest interest.

"Let's say about 10 to 15 hectares."

"My land is bigger than that. Almost twenty hectares, But half of it is occupied. You see, sir, I have once been a businessman myself. I had a technical college, a cocoa and palm oil processing mill. I had many. I took a loan from the bank and then... My property was all sold. You can look round and see what I almost became..."

2

He rose to the edge of the veranda and leaning over the railings asked Akroma to step into the yard and see. The visitor looked round with a shrug of grim satisfaction. Not that he was interested in what the man was showing him. He was merely concerned with the impression his assessment was going to make. Everything about the estate bore testimony to the fact that he had run into very serious problems somewhere down the line. Much looked abandoned, little finished! The building in which they were living had once been intended for a three-storey building. It never rose above the ground floor. The walled fence within which he lived was only partially complete. The gate was only half built. There were two old 20-ton trucks and a Land Rover, both out of use. There was even a tractor."

"Would you like to sell this property?" Akroma inquired.

"Sell? Who is there to buy?" Sabbas inquired. And then he added. "Of course, if there is somebody to buy it, why not sell it? Why should I sit by a river and use spittle to wash my hands? Why did you ask, sir?'

"Because I am interested," Akroma responded. J-P wiped his mouth. "Do you owe people on this land? Excuse me for asking you all these questions so soon because I am out here on business and I do not want to waste any minute of my time."

Pa Sabbas laughed, slapped his thighs with his palms and said: "I will answer all your questions right now. If my answers will answer my problems, why should I complain about questions? As you asked, I owe the company from which I borrowed money to start the projects. I also owe a few people."

"About how much?"

Sabbas looked at J-P and then at Akroma

"Tell him Pa," J-P said. "You think it is a joke?" He himself could hardly believe what he was beholding.

"Let's go back into the house," Sabbas said.

They all went in. After reflecting for about three minutes Sabbas said, "I think my indebtedness on this property must not be less than 46 million francs."

He was looking at the visitor as he spoke, and was impressed when he noticed that the figure quoted did not seem to disturb him.

"How much is the property itself worth?"

"Let's say about 200 million."

Akroma nodded, took out his notebook, took down a few points and then said:

"I do not have much time to be here, but it seems you have what I am looking for. I need four things done almost immediately. Do you have a Land Certificate for the land?"

"I have,. But it is with the lawyer who drew up the deed between me and my creditors."

"No problem," the visitor said. "Kojo and Sons can pre-pay them so as to transfer the document to the lawyer who will draw up the deed between you and us. We shall need the service of a computer assessor who will evaluate your property including the movable items. I guess there might be some machines there which we can revitalise and use."

"No problem, Sir, I can even go there this night…." He turned to J-P: "My son, you know that you are my God? I thought I was already a dead man. Touch my vein and you will hear that I am breathing like a normal man again."

J-P smiled, a mixture of disbelief and amazement. But he took the credit. "God's time is the best,": he said. "Man no die man no rotten."

Akroma went on: "I also require, as soon as possible, a certificate of total indebtedness'. We would want to clear all debts owing before we start. We would not like to have people come along to disturb us once we have started work. Kojo and Sons is a very serious corporation."

"It sounds serious to me," Sabbas said.

"Last but not the least, we would like you to pay a participation fee of 500,000 francs."

"I am listening," Sabbas said.

"Once that is done I shall submit my report to our technical committee which will then recommend that funds be placed at my disposal for commencement of the work."

It was Pa Sabbas himself who suggested a warm bath for both men, to show his appreciation of what he was beholding.

Chapter Twenty-Two

(Wednesday, May 23rd, 1984)

Pa Sabbas did not inquire to know any further what exactly *Kojo and Sons* intended to set up. He was too excited to ask any questions. He had suffered so much that news of resurrection such as this was bound to put reason and caution behind him. Within one week he was able to obtain all the required documents.

"Now it is only the participation fee that is left. Once that is paid we will be able to work out the percentage of involvement, whether you are coming in on a fifty-fifty basis or sixty-forty. What all this means is that we shall have to agree on the percentage of shares for each of us, considering that I am bringing in money and the personnel."

Pa Sabbas was hardly paying any more attention. He was lost in the figures that criss-crossed his mind.

2

Sebastian Nganpior's participation fee of 500,000 francs was paid on Wednesday July 4th. To raise the money the man was forced to do what he had vowed never to do – sell land earmarked for the children. There was a piece of land behind his abandoned mill, half of which he had sold to solve some of his financial problems.

"You will never solve all those your financial problems," his wife told him once. "If you think you can sell the land to solve them then you will have to sell all of it. And even if you have sold all of it, they will remain unsolved. So leave this land alone for your three children. I do not think in your absence the people you owe will treat your children with the same harshness. Leave their land alone."

He had promised never to sell any piece of it any more. The arrival of Kojo Hanson and all that he seemed determined to do compelled him to raise money by all means. Nobody was willing to lend him any money.

The sale which would normally have fetched him about two million francs, was virtually given away for 900,000 francs. Pa Sabbas had not touched that kind of money for over five years. He gave Hanson 500,000 francs as his participation fee in the Kojo Hanson and Sons Enterprise. With the 400,000 francs left, his life style changed overnight. For one thing, he saw money coming. Within months all his debts shall have been paid. His total assets had been estimated by an expert at 227 million francs. It was agreed between them that since Sabbas had no money, and since Kojo Hanson would supply the entire financing, Sabbas would be entitled to one third of the 227 million francs which he could decide to plough back in as an investment capital. Alternatively, he could invest the money in a bank and live on its interest while Kojo Hanson ran its business undisturbed.

3

During the period that Sabbas was looking for the money Akroma tried to study his new environment. Sabbas had two taxis from which he eked out a living. J-P offered to drive one for his uncle. On the 31st May therefore, J-P began driving for his uncle. Hanson said it would facilitate his prospecting enormously if one of the vehicles was placed at his disposal.

Sabbas immediately accepted, even offering to fuel the car for his visitor.

Sabbas complained about the unscrupulous nature of the taxi men. "They work 10,000 francs, give you 2,000 francs and even ask you to fuel the car for them."

"I'll solve the problem," Hanson said. He discussed the matter with J-P whom he encouraged to take over the driving of the taxi and ensure that Sabbas got as such of the money J-P worked as possible. That would justify his stay in Sabbas' house.

A few days after the taxi was placed at the disposal of Kojo Hanson for prospecting, the latter asked the original driver to teach him how to drive. He had actually learned some driving long ago and so it did not take him a week to master it. He kept the driver by his side for another week, during which time Petit-Pierre, the driver showed him round the town.

As soon as Hanson was sure that he had understood the town very well, he dismissed Petit-Pierre and took over the driving himself. He joined J-P in the taxi business, justifying this decision by telling Sabbas that while waiting for a reply from Liberia he could not just sit back and watch. He said he would help raise some money for Sabbas. And he really did. The two men gave Sabbas 14,000 francs each night, an act which endeared him all the more to them.

Hanson drove for two months and then, seeing how much money he could make, he made a suggestion to Sabbas. He said the man could turn his taxi over to him as part of his investment when the company finally took off. He told Sabbas to decide on a cost that would benefit him.

"Since it will be me to work out and sign the final documents, do not be afraid to quote any figure which you think would be to your advantage in future. How much should the car cost here now?"

"Two Million francs," Sabbas said.

"Turn it in for Five million francs, and I will sign that I accepted the car on behalf of the company for that much, which sum goes in as part of your investment capital"

Pa Sabbas was extremely happy to hand over his old car for the projected sum of five million francs. He did not mention this deal to his wife. He believed that she was too dull and too short-sighted to see any advantage in sacrificing present pleasure for future gains.

Chapter Twenty-Three

(Monday June 25th, 1984)

The acquisition of a car was not all that Akroma did. His taxi work ended at 6p.m each day. He had already applied to teach English in some evening schools that were preparing students for the Baccalaureate and other examinations. After carefully studying the setup of all the colleges around, he decided that he could make his future at *Cours du Soir Anguissa-Anguissa.* On the 25th of June he made a breakthrough - he gained employment as English Language teacher in that institution.

The proprietor of the college, Anguissa-Anguissa Bertin was, as Akroma went all out to discover, a local millionaire. Like many of his kind, his whole life was devoted to making money and saving it. He saw human beings, whatever their educational level, whatever their natural endowments, as tools to be used for acquiring wealth and then being dumped when the services had been squeezed from them. He would go to any extent to enlist the services of a good driver, cook, teacher or business manager. But once he had gotten what he wanted from the man, rather than pay for the services rendered, he would trump up a charge against the employee and cause him to leave in frustration. Workers he was owing were known to have been arrested and locked up on one charge or another.

2

He never spared an opportunity to enrich himself at the expense of anybody. He personally did his banking, and so nobody knew just how much he had in the banks, But everybody knew that he was extremely rich. He had three wives and fourteen children. Three of the children, a boy and two girls were studying in the University. But, living in constant fear of being killed by either his wives or children in order to possess his wealth, he trusted nobody. He visited nobody, never shared a drink with anybody and never permitted anybody to serve him a drink, water or food. He prepared his meals himself.

He could not have been less than sixty-five years old by a day. Slightly shorter than Akroma he was a man of very massive stature: a very large, bald, oval head, a stunted nose that looked like God had stuck a black table tennis ball to its tip, large harmless eyes with heavy upper lids.

He was a great snuff-taker with evidence of this always seen trickling unpicturesquely from his cavernous nostrils. The mouth was equally large with thick, red, upturned lips. He never went to school, but by dint of hard work and much luck, he had amassed a lot of wealth. It had taken the managers of the local banks several months to teach him how to draw two interlocking circles and draw a line through them by way of signing this signature. And even when, he did it differently each time he signed for money. But he more than compensated for his lack of education with an instinct to smell treachery and money. He could tell the sound of his vehicle even when nobody else seemed to hear anything. Akroma saw in him a veritable farm to exploit and quickly set to work.

When he began teaching his course, the proprietor promised him 1500 francs per hour and he was to teach five hours a week. That would have given him 30,000 francs per month. At the end of that very first month he was paid only 20,000 francs. He accepted without a demure, an act which endeared him to Bertin, especially because Akroma was said to be a very knowledgeable and devoted teacher.

The scheming Akroma was bidding his time. An accomplished artist, he taught drawing free to the students who were interested in art. He even made a pencil portrait of the proprietor which he framed and presented to the old man – free of charge. Anguissa-Anguissa was very pleased.

3

Slowly but steadily Akroma penetrated the hermetically sealed world of Anguissa-Anguissa, and before long he had completely ingratiated himself into the old man's favour. This he did mainly by making himself what Anguissa-Anguissa liked to see: an enormously talented, well- educated, tireless and obliging fool. He visited Anguissa-Anguissa whenever he could and discussed ways of improving the college. Once when he visited Anguissa-Anguissa he found the man performing a ridiculous act: he was sitting in front to an artistic structure whose presence in the house had always puzzled him. The two-metre high and two–metre wide structure which was made of wood comprised of two intersecting circles with a line running through the point of intersection. The old man sat in front of the image with a piece of paper before him. He seemed to be trying to copy the image.

Anguissa-Anguissa was preparing to go and do some banking and was in fact practising how to sign his signature. The banks respected him as an invaluable customer, but were embarrassed by the fact that he could not sign any signature twice, however simple it was. Even the two circles still posed problems to him.

Chapter Twenty-Four

(Tuesday, July 10th 1984)

Akroma regarded Anguissa-Anguissa as a sacred book that needed to be studied thoroughly. And study it he did! When he had convinced himself that he had read and understood the book he decided to submit himself to the test. On Tuesday the 10th of July he went up to Anguissa-Anguissa and asked him why he could not convert the evening school into a regular college.

"I hear it is very difficult to do so," the old man told him, rubbing his protruding forehead with his left hand. "I hear to do it you will bribe and bribe and it will not work."

"Has anybody here tried it?"

"No."

"Let me try. Let me find out what it costs to try."

Morbidly sensitive to exploitation and the motives of anybody towards him, the old man took out his snuff box and drew in several nailfuls. He thanked Akroma for his kindness in thinking so and gave him his blessings. He was convinced it would not work.

2

Akroma got the vital facts from the Delegation of the Ministry of Education the very next day. There was a set of dossiers to be completed in triplicate. Upon submission there was going to be an inspection by a team from the delegation. The proprietor's assets were to be assessed and the structures checked to ensure that they suited the purpose. There was also going to be a morality report sent by the Commissaries for Special Branch, to ascertain that they were not dealing with a crook who would swindle parents and students and then escape.

Each of these steps entailed a bribe of at least 50,000 francs. The whole exercise would cost about 300,000 francs. Thereafter the dossiers would be sent to Yaounde where the Director of Private Education would study and make his recommendations to the Minister of Education. To speed up things in Yaounde, somebody told him in confidence, he would need to give the Director of Private Education an envelope of about 100,000francs .

Njonjo returned to Anguissa – Anguissa with his findings and the figures which would benefit him.

"It is possible for you to have a full-fledged college here within six weeks, in fact, by the beginning of the next school year."

As could have been expected, the old man doubted every word of it. At any rate he listened.

"It boils down to money," the wily Njonjo said, "You don't do anything. You simply make the money available, and then you will go on records as The Proprietor of Lycee. No. I. Classique Polyvalent de Nijombari."

"How much money is that?"

"If you go to the Delegation yourself, since they know you have money, you will spend about 500,000 francs."

"I am not going anywhere. Since they know that I cannot read and write, they will always want to cheat me. You will do the running about."

"With 300,000 francs I can get the Delegate to sign. But mark you," he cautioned. " You will not give me more money than we need at any one time. You will only give as the situation requires, after each phase is complete, and while we are to engage in a new phase.

With 100,000 francs I can get the Ministry of Health to sign. With 250,000francs I can get the *Commissaire* of Special Branch to give you the best morality report. The problem is with Yaounde. We have to prepare an envelope for the Director of Private Education, we are looking at about 200,000 francs. We have also to encourage the Minister to sign. His envelope should be about 350,000francs.

Although Anguissa-Anguissa was a stark illiterate, he was excellent at figures.

"I have 1 million two hundred thousand francs in my head," he announced to Njonjo.

"Make that amount of money available to me as the situation requires, and I will give you a college anytime."

Anguissa-Anguissa reflected deeply and said:

"Come to me on Sunday evening."

3

By Saturday he had tried on his own to see how much it would cost him. The figures were a lot higher than what Njonjo had quoted. On Sunday evening Njongo showed up and when he left he had 1.3million francs in his pocket. Anguissa-Anguissa had decided to risk that amount of money. Njonjo was sure to make over 500,000francs in the deal. At one point he even thought of fleeing with the money, but he thought it was too early. He saw better days ahead if he played the honest broker.

On Wednesday July 4th Sabbas had succeeded in selling the plot, the proceeds of which he gave to Akroma as his participation fee for a company Akroma had long forgotten of. On Monday July 9th, Akroma succeeded in making him turn in his taxi as further investment.

He did not tell J-P about these other developments. He decided that he would be honest with Anguissa-Anguissa at least in the beginning, and then make quick money before escaping., He reported his progress periodically to Anguissa-Anguissa. Before he left Nijombari for Yaounde he reported, and he also did so on his return.

"There will be no problem," he reassured the old man.

"No problem whatsoever. I have plugged all the holes. But what do I get if the school is approved?"

"What will you want? You want money?"

"Well, I know you will pay me for my labour. But with the school, what position will I occupy?"

"Tell me the position."

Akroma wanted to say Bursar, but he thought that would draw suspicion onto himself. "As principal, I think I can continue to help you grow. I think, for the good of the school and for your own good, it is good for me to be principal."

" I agree," the old man said.

"But let me advise you that whenever you are employing anybody, let me know and make my own assessment…"

"Employ? You are my God. Are you not the man to employ all of them?"

"I was fearing."

4

On Monday July 6th, 1984 the amount of money necessary was made available to Akroma and he left. He was away for two weeks. On Saturday August 11th 1984 Cours du Soir Anguissa-Anguissa was granted Ministerial approval. It was also permitted to open the first and second cycles at the same time. The new name for the Institution was LYCEE CLASSIQUE NO. 1 POLYVALENT DE NIJOMBARI.

Akroma did not even need to lobby for the post of Principal, it was his. He then went on to appoint or cause the rest of the administrative staff to be employed, except the bursar who remained the proprietor's nephew.

Chapter Twenty-Five

(Nijombari, Wednesday July 11th, 1984)

Pa Sabbas Ngangpior had three children, a boy and two girls. The first two were studying in America, a decision he taken had in his heyday, when money was the least of his problems. The thought of it now haunted him because soon afterwards it became impossible for him to earn the amount of monies the children needed so badly. They plagued him with letters every month.

Immediately he struck the verbal deal with KOJO AND SONS, he wrote back to reassure his children that his sufferings were already at an end, and that they would soon start breathing fresh air again. The problem, however, came not from America, but from Cameroon. Their third child, Monique, was in the third year in the faculty of law in the University of Yaounde.. She had not finished rejoicing at the letter her father had sent to her announcing his impending wealth when her mother wrote to say her father had broken the family law by selling one of their most precious pieces of land.

2

Monique arrived Nijombari unannounced. She was convinced that her mother would be in the market, but she decided to go home and leave her *travelling* bag before going to see her in the market. She arrived her father's house at about noon. One of her father's taxis was parked outside the gate.

When she entered the house a gentle man she had never met before was emerging from one of the rooms in the corridor of the uncompleted main building. He returned to the room as soon as he saw her before coming out again to meet her. They exchanged greetings and the man seemed to know her even though he was a complete stranger to her.

The man went to stand on the veranda and he seemed to be adjusting his pair of trousers as if he had been dressing up in the room. As she passed through the corridor her mother emerged from the same room.

"Why have you come here now?" her mother asked preposterously. The question embarrassed her.

"I am no longer a child of this family, mama?"

The woman smiled and with guilt written all over her face she said:

"Why not? I am just asking because we were not expecting you."

Mama Anna called for the stranger.

"Have you met my daughter before?" she asked.

"No, Madam. Welcome," the man greeted Monique.

She answered and immediately inquired: "Who is this man, Mama?"

There was a tenseness in her voice which indicated she was not exactly asking for an introduction.

"Somebody," her mother said.

"Where is papa?" Monique asked.

"When he leaves the house can anybody ever tell where he has gone to? Is that why you are asking who is this man like that?"

"That is not the reason. I am asking two different questions."

"I don't know where your father has gone to."

Monique leaned back against the wall and looked at her mother with a worried expression on her face. She had never associated the mother with any kind of misconduct. But it was clear to her mind that her mother and whoever the man was, had been engaged in some adulterous affair.

"Who is that man, mama?" she asked again.

"I will tell you, Monique, " she said, "Don't fear, it is nothing."

Monique took in a deep breath and said: "Mama, I came to see you and to see papa too about the letter you sent to me. Did you say papa has sold that land near the stream?"

"He has."

"For how much?"

"Can he tell me such things?"

3

The explanation which Sabbas gave her when he returned in the evening reeked of swindle. "If he is such a rich investor," she argued, "why should he ask you for a participation fee? Why should you be the one to pay the assessor of your property? Why should you house him?"

There was no receipt for the money paid as participation fee.

"Participation fee for what, papa?" she shouted. "What legal documents bind you two?"

There were, in fact, no legal documents binding them. "Why would a man who is ready to pay you 227 million francs start off by being a taxi driver for you? Mineral investors are extremely rich people, who usually do not hide their identities. There are many things I want to know about that your millionaire investor who is causing you to sell everything to satisfy him."

Monique decided to trail the activities of Kojo Hanson.

4

Within forty-eight hours she had proved that her father had been victim to a dupe. There was no such person as Kojo Hanson, a Liberian investor, no such organisation as Kojo and Sons. The man who went by that name was actually Njonjo Fabian Mula, a Cameroonian, born in Tiko and who had studied in Ghana. That same person whom she had found under very suspicious circumstances with her mother was now the director of studies of College No .1 Classique de Nijombari.

It was not even necessary to inform Pa Sabbas that he was being cuckolded. This news, coupled with the loss incurred in the sale of the land and the car he had given away broke Pa Sabbas heart. He developed instant high blood pressure. That evening he had a stroke and by the morning he was already a corpse.

Monique reported the matter to the police. But it was a wasted effort. Mula, as the man was popularly known, was already too popular. He was the Police, and it was his own explanation that was taken. Upon hearing that he, Njonjo, had studied in Ghana, Sabbas had tried to see if they could set up a joint-project in mineral prospecting. He had agreed, but when he found that it was hard-going and not profitable he had abandoned the exercise. As for the car, he had legal documents to show that it had been sold to him. Case dismissed!.

Part Three

Chapter Twenty-Six

It was Akroma's excesses that undid him. By June 1985, Akroma had already made enough money to solve all his problems in Ghana. He made at least 3 million francs from the KOJO AND SONS ENTERPRISE speculation, including the car. He made 1.7 million francs from the approval of the school. Since he was in charge of employment, he made 3 million francs from bribes from job seekers. In some cases people bribed but were never employed. He gave them promises which he was not under any obligation to keep.

During the Christmas break in Mid December 1984 he visited Ghana. He was all money. He had the sum of 3 million francs stitched into the shoulders of his coat and over coat. He had 2 million francs sewn in the sole of a pair of shoes specially made for that purpose. He had 500,000 francs stitched into the inner lining of a large leather belt. Using his Cameroonian identity card he entered Nigeria through Ikok and used the same identity card to travel to the Nigerian/Benin border. He had no visa to enter Nigeria, but he had enough money to solve the problem Thence he used his Ghanaian passport all the way to Lome.

When he converted his francs into New Cedis in Lome he had with him 42,000 New Cedis. Within a week all the debts they owed the Bank of Commerce were cleared. He would have died a rich man if he had decided to set up some form of business with such a capital. But he thought he had not milked Cameroon enough.

2

By the middle of January 1985, he was back in Nijombari using the same route. At the Cameroon/ Nigeria border he simply showed his Cameroonian identity and he was permitted to enter. He had long employed J-P as the college driver. At the beginning of the second year in October he decided on the deal that would crown his efforts and send him back to Ghana an absolute millionaire.

He invited the bursar of the college for a drink three times. The third time he asked bursar:

"Why are you here?"

"Why do you ask?"

"No, just tell me. You are here to work, not so?"

"To earn a living," the bursar said. "To help my uncle," he added.

"No," Njonjo said, "the most important thing is to earn a living. You went to school, right?"

The man nodded.

"People went to school to organise their lives. The national campaign for education will not bear any fruits until we have made people regret who have never been to school"

The bursar seemed to guess what the man was driving at. He leaned forward and supported his chin in his left hand.

"Patron can't read or write," Njonjo went on. "He can only count his money. Meanwhile he was supposed to have been to school. He did not. It is the greatest of all human tragedies for an educated man's life to be placed at the mercy of a confirmed illiterate. God forbid! Let us reap the benefit of our education by teaching him a lesson.. I have told him that the enrolment for this year is 2000. But as you know, the records shows 3000. We collect fees for the other 1000 students and we share them between ourselves."

He got away with this too. But he was not satisfied. He made deals with suppliers, got huge sums of money to give contracts to suppliers.

Chapter Twenty-Seven

(Wednesday,18th February, 1986)

On Wednesday the 18th of February 1986, the Director of Private Education visited Lycee Classique Polyvalent No.1 de Nijombari on a routine tour. Just as he had done in the other colleges, he discussed problems between private colleges and the Government administration and made suggestions for improvement. As far as this particular college was concerned, he was impressed by the performance of the students at the public examinations. He praised the level of discipline, but complained about the absence of certain key infrastructures such as a play ground and toilet facilities for both boys and girls. He drew the attention of the proprietor and principal to the fact that it was wrong for the students and teachers to share the same pit latrine.

"We will create all that," the proprietor said with undisguised agitation. "Our main problem is that the Government had reduced the subventions, and so we depend only on enrolment for money. This is a new school, and as numbers increase we will make life better for our students..."

The Director was not convinced.

"I can understand," he began, "If you were the proprietor of a school of 100 or less. With an enrolment of 3000 and over," he shook his head, "this is unacceptable."

There was a long, tense silence during which Anguissa-Anguissa looked from his principal to the Director with obvious resentment.

"Who said we have 3000 students, my Director?" he inquired.

"It is written down in black and white," the Director said. Akroma nudged the Director with his right elbow. The man, instinctively sensed that there was a problem. It was Akroma himself who continued.

"Patron," he began with a nervous ingratiating smile, "what the director is saying is that this school has the potential to hold 3000 students and more, and that we need that number to be able to improve on our standards. I hope I have got you right?" he turned to the Director with a persuasive wink which the man did not miss.

"Of course," he said. "Of course."

Anguissa-Anguissa was a man of extra-sensory perception when it came to matters of money. He seemed lost in what he was beholding.

2

Akroma closed the meeting suddenly with an invitation to lunch which he had caused to be prepared. He stuck close to the Director, and while Anguissa-Anguissa was still ruminating on the implications of what had just transpired, he told the visitor.

"We have a problem with admission numbers, as you can see, Mr. Director. I will explain to you."

He seemed prepared to welcome the Director because before they sat down for their sumptuous meal, Akroma smuggled an envelope into the Director's ready hands. Half way through the meal the Director asked and was shown the way to the toilet. Five minutes later he returned, all smiles. He was one million francs richer. He did the talking throughout the rest of the meal. He encouraged the proprietor to pay his staff regularly, so as to maintain the high standard that would increase intake. He said he was impressed by the way things were going, and that in five years there was no reason why the school would not be able to register an enrolment of 3000.

Chapter Twenty-Eight

(Monday March 25th, 1986)

The Director of Private Education had accepted the bribe without protest. Here and there he discovered a bursar or a principal who played pranks on their proprietors. But nowhere else did he find anybody or persons exploiting the ignorance or illiteracy of a proprietor to that alarming extent. He could not visit all the private colleges, but he believed that there must be some in which the same malpractice existed. Upon that assumption he decided to send out his agents to investigate. He sent out a circular to the provincial presidents for Lay-Private Education, ordering them to undertake a tour of all their colleges along lines suggested.

2

When on Tuesday March, 1986 the proprietor of Lycee Classique Polyvalent No.1 de Nijombari received a note from the President of Lay-Private Education announcing his visit the following week, he handed it over to his principal. Having silenced the Director of Private Education during his last visit to Nijombari, Akroma was anxious to follow that up by winning every other authority who was likely to stir up trouble, to his side. He therefore encouraged Anguissa-Anguissa to apply to host the impending workshop.

3

While Akroma's empire and popularity grew as his days in Nijombari stretched out, other persons also improved in their various jobs. On Monday August 27th 1984, Inspector Kum Dangobert was admitted in the Police College in Yaounde for a nine-month course. When he returned on Tuesday June 25th, 1985, as *Officier de Police de Troisième Grade*, he was made Commanding Officer of *19ème Arrondisement* in Douala.

On Sunday March 31st 1985 too, a general meeting of the churches met which was attended by parents whose children attended Mission schools. At the end of that event a new executive was appointed to run Lay-Private Education. A certain Mr. Ambroise Bilong Emana was voted President. Reverend Dieudonne Akwa was voted the Vice-President. When the Director of Private Education's circular was received at the Provincial Office in Douala, Mr. Emana lay dying from a stroke he suffered two months before. As the constitution stipulated, under such circumstances, he was to be represented on the tour by his Vice-President, Reverend Dieudonne Akwa.

"There was also a radio announcement to that effect," Reverend Dieudonne Akwa added.

4

When Dangobert returned from his training in Yaounde, one of the first persons he contacted was Reverend Dieudonne Akwa. When he inquired whether Akwa had received any further news concerning Akroma and J-P, Reverend Dieudonne Akwa showed him a newspaper cutting he had made in September the previous year. It read:

OBITUARY

The unclaimed bodies of two men, Mombangui Jean-Paul, holder of Cameroonian National Identity Card No. 07965/B who hails from Biongong, and Mr. Patrickston Essuman Akroma, holder of Ghanaian passport No. Pa/785634, who hails from Accra in Ghana, both victims of the fatal accident of Friday, September 14th, 1984 at Mulundu have been buried by the Mulundu municipal council cemetery.

There was a radio announcement to that effect," Reverend Dieudonne Akwa added.

Commissaire Dangobert seemed to doubt the news.

"These Ghanaians," he said, "are capable of anything. Remember it took us all out effort to establish Akroma was not the one who got burned in that hotel? Anyway, let us give them the benefit of the doubt and accept that they are dead. At least it will make us sleep soundly." And there the matter ended, or seemed to end. *Commissaire* Dangobert's instincts were not at fault. That obituary had been sent in by Akroma himself just to keep the police off his back.

Chapter Twenty-Nine

(Thursday March 20st, 1986)

On Thursday March 20st at 9am a black Peugeot 504 drove into the college compound. It halted very briefly in front of the Administrative block, asked for the way to the Proprietor's office and then drove off. As the car drove towards the Proprietors' house J-P ran into Akroma's office through the back door and said:

"Monsieur Le Directeur, die has come to us."

"What do you mean, J-P?"

Panting with trepidation. J-P lowered his head and told him conspiratorially: "That man we are waiting for is Reverend Dieudonne Akwa. Trouble has come."

"How do you know?" he asked, vainly fighting to conceal his own apprehension.

"How can I not know Reverend Akwa?' J-P asked.

"Did he see you?" Akroma inquired worriedly.

"I sure, *Monsieur Le Directeur.* Run you away."

Akroma ran his hands over this head and then cleaned his eyes with both hands.

"I am not running away, J-P" he said. "Instead you run and hide. I am the one to talk first at the meeting. If he discovers me I will convince him that I am not the man he thinks he knows. After the meeting we can plan how to get away…"

2

J-P went out through the same back door of the office just as the black Peugeot 504 drove back to the Administrative block. The proprietor was driving behind them. The authorities of the other colleges who had been waiting around the entrance came down immediately and joined the staff of Lycee Classique No. 1 de Nijombari. They all stood in a line, members of the delegations from the various colleges sticking together. The proprietor, principals, vice principals and bursars of five other colleges were on hand to receive him.

"Mr. Njonjo Fabian Mula, from Tiko Sub Division in the Southern West Province, my Principal," Anguissa-Anguissa said to the visitor, pointing to Akroma by way of introduction. He then asked the other proprietors to introduce their representatives.

The visitor shook hands with each person as he was being introduced to him. Akroma was careful to keep his head lowered, averting any possible scrutiny on the part of Akwa. They all strolled gently into the conference room that had been prepared for the occasion.

There the visitor introduced himself as Reverend Pastor Dieudonne Akwa who was sitting in for Mr. Emana who was very sick. He told them he had come in late the previous night and had checked into Etoile Philante, one of the big hotels in the small town.

3

Just as he drove into the college campus, Reverend Dieudonne Akwa had caught a glimpse of somebody who resembled his former driver J-P who had been on the run for about two years. That glimpse of J-P made him curious to know more about the place and the people. In his anxious and irascible mind he had come to the uncharitable conclusion that if J-P were around there, then his accomplice, Akroma, long presumed dead, must not be too far away. He therefore decided to keep his eyes wide open for any clues.

So when Anguissa-Anguissa introduced his principal to him, in spite of the enormous disguise, Reverend Dieudonne Akwa's eyes came to rest unwaveringly on the man. He thought there was something of the long-sought-for Akroma in the Principal's bearing. It was something remote, sharpened mainly by the fact that he had sighted J-P. Yet it was there. He remembered that Akroma had a mole on his left jaw.

However, as soon as they had settled down for business he introduced the purpose of his meeting. "I am here on the orders of the Minister of National Education to investigate a few things." He read the circular from the Director:

Figures of enrolment numbers submitted to the Ministry do not reflect the realities in the field. Some unscrupulous proprietors, in order to increase their subventions, inflate the numbers of students. Even worse, certain unscrupulous principals conceal the actual figures of student enrolments from their proprietors, thereby amassing huge sums of monies for themselves…

In spite of his religious upbringing, Reverend Dieudonne Akwa was an unusually emotional personality who usually found it hard to camouflage or suppress his feelings on things that hurt him. The thought of J-P around there so unsettled him that he suddenly lost interest in the meeting and instead thought he had better track down the fugitive first.

After presenting his programme he was looking round when his eyes came to rest suspiciously again on the man the proprietor had introduced at Njonjo Fabian Mula, the Principal of Lycee Classique Polyvalent No. 1 de Nijombari. The visitor looked at the principal and then gazed deeply and meditatively into space as though he contemplated a great shining vision.

"I may be wrong," he said, probing the man's figure with unapologetic interest. "but it would appear we have met before."

"I am not sure," the man said flatly, his mind pulsing so hard and fast that only a series of deep breaths restored his equilibrium. At least for the moment.

"Never before?" he inquired , throwing a casual glance on his left jaw where he found the tell-tale mole which the nest of beard had not succeeded in concealing , a significant detail which Akroma had forgotten to take care of.

"Never in my life," the principal said. "Not to the best of my knowledge," he emphasised with a heart that seemed to beat above his fast breathing. "I am Mula Njonjo Fabian, I hail from Tiko in the South West Province. Whom did you think you were talking to, sir?"

Reverend Akwa's dull but honest countenance flushed darkly and uneasily. He looked at Akroma for a while, forced a brief smile, shook his head and said:

"This is the programme. I will try to see a few of the schools this afternoon. Tomorrow morning at 3 pm, we will meet here again so that I discuss my findings with everybody present."

The discovery of Akroma and J-P seemed right then more important to him than the mission. Unable to contain his indignation he rose and immediately taking an excuse went to his car without telling them what schools he would be visiting and at what time. As an afterthought he came back, called for Anguissa-Anguissa and asked whether his college had a driver.

"Ah-ah. Mr. President, A whole college like this will not have a driver? We have three."

"Let me see them all," Reverend Dieudonne Akwa said. Anguissa–Anguissa thought the need to see the drivers was part of the President's research. He called for the Principal and asked him to send for the drivers.

Only two turned up. J-P was at large. Neither Anguissa-Anguissa nor the other participants had the slightest inkling of the drama that was unfolding before their own eyes.

Chapter Thirty

(Thursday March 20st, 1986)

Reverend Dieudonne Akwa drove straight back to his hotel, Etoile Philante. As soon as he got to his room he telephoned *the 19ème Arrondissement* in Douala and asked to talk to *Commissaire* Kum Dangobert. When the man got on the phone Akwa introduced himself and immediately said:

"I am phoning from Nijombari. I got here last night and I have made two crucial encounters which I think it would interest you to know."

"I am listening, Pastor," Dangobert said.

"The driver of the college here is none other than my own J-P whom we thought dead."

Dangobert smacked his lips.

"That's not all," Akwa went on. "I was to meet the principals, proprietors and bursars of five colleges here. At the working session this morning, I met a gentleman whom I could have sworn was that our wanted Akroma fellow."

"Does he bear the same names?" Dangobert inquired.

"Not at all. Now he goes by the names Njonjo Mula Fabian, or something of the sort, said to have been born in Tiko in the South West Province."

Dangobert wrote down something and then said pointedly:

"I am sure he recognised you."

"Of course he must have."

"Did you give him the impression that you recognised him?'

"I didn't," Akwa lied.

"Raise no alarm, then. Proceed with your meeting as if you noticed nothing. By the way, for how long were you supposed to be in Nijombari?"

"It is for me to decide. It could all end in a day, the way I feel now. The sight of this crook upsets me terribly…"

"Stretch it for as long as you can," Dangobert advised. "I'll get in touch with my elements both here and over there and see how to get at him. The same thing applies to your driver. Ignore him and go about your business. We'll surprise them both."

Chapter Thirty-One

(Friday, March 21st, 1986)

Commissaire Dangobert spent Thursday afternoon working out a plan to surprise Akroma and his friend in their lair. He would inform Akwa to secretly get more information on Akroma, where he lived and places he frequented and at what times. He would then get in touch with the *Commissaire* of Public Security and hint him on the matter. He would then tell Akwa to return to Douala with precise information on how to locate both Akroma and J-P. He would then go to Nijombari with his elements for the final onslaught.

He started trying phoning Etoile Philante de Nijombari at 5 o'clock, but each time he dialled it was the same message that was received.

"Due to traffic conditions, please call later." He assigned a policeman to the task while he continued with other duties in his office. At 7pm the policeman reported that the call had finally gone through.

He introduced himself and asked to speak to Reverend Dieudonne Akwa.

"We have a very big problem here, Monsieur Le *Commissaire*," the speaker said. "Reverend Akwa was discovered dead in his room this morning. The people are saying that he was killed. That is what they are calling the police to talk about."

When Dangobert inquired further the man explained what they knew: when the hotel attendant came to clean Reverend Akwa's room and to inquire about his breakfast, the door was locked. Looking through the half-opened louvers he raised an alarm. The door was broken and Reverend Akwa found dead, murdered.'

All fingers pointed at the night watchman. He said that the only strange person who came in that evening was a lady who said she had been invited by Reverend Akwa. At first he swore that he had been at the gate all night and that he had not seen her leave the hotel premises. Later, as the accusations mounted he confessed that he had returned to his house at mid night. His wife and children had supported what he had said. He would lose his job on that score, but for the moment, the problem was, 'who killed Reverend Akwa?"

2

After the murder the assailant had locked the door from outside and thrown the key inside through the half-open louvers.

One of the important personalities to appear at the scene that morning was Akroma. He looked just as outraged as everybody else. *Commissaire* Essomba received the news just when he got to the office at 8.30 that morning. But the news had been in circulation for a full hour. In fact, a Gendarme and a policeman had each passed by just as the alarm was being raised. The policeman as well as the Gendarme had told the people to make a report and affix a 500 francs fiscal stamp to it and submit to the main office.

The Gendarmes had responded faster, such that when Essomba eventually arrived at 10am, he found Gendarmes interrogating the hotel workers. This brought the perennial antagonism between the two forces to the fore, with each claiming jurisdiction!

"You call me up," he shouted, "and while I am getting ready to come, you call in the Gendarmes. What are you trying to prove?"

The Gendarmes abandoned the scene and went away. Essomba also went away, cursing. As he went away, Akroma playing the role of the good citizen, drew the manager of the hotel and told him:

"This kind of thing can spoil your business. This thing that they are saying that the man was killed, will kill business from this hotel."

The man ground his teeth, pulled at his beard and then asked:

"So what do I do, sir?"

The perversity that had bedevilled his entire wretched life impelled him to shrug his shoulders slightly and say: "You have to convince the *Commissaire* to say something different. You have to encourage him to tell the doctor to say he died by some other means…"

3

Etoile, for so the manager was commonly called, went into his office for a while and, returning out, immediately took after Essomba . Arriving Essomba's office the man pleaded. First he persuaded Essomba to sent his men to look into the matter. When Essomba complained of transport Etoile gave 5,000 francs.

He then stretched his hand and gave Essomba an envelope."

"What do you have here?" Essomba asked with far less severity. "A convocation?" He tore the envelope open and counted the notes.

"They kill a man in your hotel and you give me. 50,000 francs?"

The man looked round, shut the door and said in a whisper: "Put it in your pocket, Monsieur Le *Commissaire*. I run the hotel. If news goes round that a man has been killed in that hotel, I shall be put out of business...*Commissaire*, I want you to carry out the investigations yourself. Let the world hear that the man died himself, not that he was killed. While my business is going on, you can then begin to carry out the investigations of the real cause of his death…"

"But I am not the doctor," Essomba said.

"I know, Monsieur Le *Commissaire*. I am going to talk to the doctor too."

And go he did! For the sum of 100,000 francs. Dr. Okoladik decided on the spot, even without seeing the corpse, that Reverend Dieudonne Akwa had died of cardiac arrest. The corpse was later removed to the mortuary for a routine autopsy before it was dispatched to Douala for burial in a sealed coffin.

That saved the hotel and also drew suspicion away from the true killer. But not for long, and not from everybody's point of view.

Chapter Thirty-Two

(Friday, March 21st, 1986)

No single incident had shocked as many people as the murder of the pastor. Such a thing had never happened before in Nijombari. Not that there had never been murders! But each time a man was killed the motive was clear- robbery. Within living memory, the clergy had never been the target of thieves, especially a clergy from such an obscure organisation as LICE.

Dangobert swore to himself that the man Akwa saw was Akroma himself, and that he must have been killed either by Akroma or J-P. But his intuition told him that it was Akroma who must have done so to conceal any discovery.

J-P learned of the death of Reverend Akwa at 10 am. Although he was fleeing from Reverend Akwa, the death so outraged him that he was unable to hide his feelings. There was only one person he knew who could have killed the pastor. That one person was Akroma. He could not explain why he thought so, or how it could have happened. But he had come to believe that there was no known evil Akroma could not practise.

At 12 noon he went to Akroma's office, entered and shut the door. "*Directeur* heard that Reverend Akwa has been killed?"

"Killed?" Akroma exclaimed. "Poor man. How can they kill a man like that? Such a God man!"

J-P scratched his head, tightened his lips and said:

"*Directeur*, let me vomit my heart to you."

"What?"

"I have been following you since we left Douala and I have tried my best to help you. In doing so I think God has also been on our side. If not they would have caught us and imprisoned us long long ago. Now you have turned to the side of Satan, why Monsieur Le Directeur?"

"I don't understand what you are saying, my friend J-P."

"Monsieur Le Directeur, it was what you did that caused my uncle Pa Sabbas to die before his own day," J-P said, poisonous hatred and a wild repulsion stamped on his visage.

"What has that got to do with Reverend Akwa's death?"

"*Monsieur Le Directeur*, I want also to tell you that you killed Reverend Akwa, or you sent somebody to kill him."

"Why would I do such a thing?"

"That is what I also came to ask you, *Monsieur Le Directeur*."

"If you say that again to anybody else, J-P, you will no longer be my friend," Akroma said.

It was no advice, it was a threat, a warning, for him to keep his mouth shut. J-P recalled the day years ago when Akroma asked him in a voice full of like threats, to help him remain in Cameroon. With that thought he lifted his eyes and looked into Akroma's satanic countenance. His eyes had suddenly turned devilishly fiery and inhumanly cold. He got the message.

"How can I be saying that to anybody else?" he inquired nervously. "I said so because I was talking to you."

Chapter Thirty-Three

Once he was sure that he had by the fake *CAMEROON TRIBUNE* and radio announcement, convinced his pursuers that he was dead, Akroma set out to consolidate his financial strength – his main reason for coming to Cameroon in the first place. This consolidation, he figured, was dependent on the degree of security he would have to enjoy. The security, in turn, depended on the calibre of friends he would have to make.

The first and most decisive opportunity to win friends of substance occurred during the period he sought Ministerial approval for Anguissa-Anguissa's college. That exercise brought him into direct contact with the Delegates for Health, Education and Lands, the *Procureur de La Republique*, the President of the High Court, the Divisional Chief of National Security and the Magistrates.

Each of these contacts involved a huge financial expense. Since Anguissa-Anguissa was anxious to see his college approved, since he had made enough money available to Akroma, and since Akroma himself knew how much he stood to make from any deal with the authorities, Akroma spent substantially on them. Kindness and generosity became the keystones of everything, his career and his life. He knew very early that if he placed his favours at the disposal of highly-placed individuals, nobody would be terribly anxious to find out about his past. Whatever else he was doing, whether he was wooing Sabba's wife or outwitting Anguissa-Anguissa, he took exquisite care to preserve that image of a good man which he had created in Nijombari. And he protected it with cunning.

For instance, the Delegate of Health had asked for 50,000 francs. Akroma took 150, francs from Anguissa-Anguissa, but gave the Delegate 60,000 francs. In each case he made at least 100,000 francs. He knew that in the event of his true identity being discovered, he would need the intervention of all these personalities. Thus, even after the approval had been granted to the college, he continued to impress them all. He never missed an important even in which he could strengthen his relationship with the powers that be. If he heard of a death, a birth, a promotion celebration or a graduation ceremony in any family of significance, he did not only attend but brought a conspicuous gift. On national feasts like 11th February and 20th May, he personally brought Champagnes to each important Government Official. He was known all over as most generous individual. So popular was he that many well-placed Cameroonians had to pass through him to obtain favours or services from the police or the legal department.

He threw parties to which he invited the important government officials. The "*born-house*" of his first child, Bonaventure was attended by a *virtual who is who* in Nijombari! On record he maintained the identity card that had been fabricated in Douala showing that he was called Njonjo Fabian Mula, born at Tiko and resident in Douala.

2

Of all the relationships he made, and the one which he most valued and needed, it was that he struck with a perpetual ineabriate, Mouralais Essomba Prusmbit, alias "Ninja", the Divisional Chief of National Security for Nijombari.

Just a little over a metre and a half in height, with a roundish f ace and squinted eyes which many said had been caused by alcohol, Prusmbit was a two-star officer whom everybody considered a public nuisance, but who had risen to the rank of *Commissaire* mainly because the Minister of Defence was an uncle of his.

He was dark in complexion, scarcely ever combed his hair or shaved his beard, and wore an old pair of spectacles with lenses so scratched that you wondered how he saw through them and why he thought he needed them in the first place. He was so often in uniform that a casual observer would think he loved his job very much. Perhaps he actually loved the job so much, since it brought him so much drink, but the main reason he wore the uniform so often was because in it he was sure to squeeze a drink from almost anybody. He drank and smoked incessantly and was very popular among harlots.

There was no major vice he was not known to have committed. He had been discovered under a mask when a team of armed robbers had been trapped. Had led a gang to way-lay a businessman who had "*chopped njangi*". He had been involved in money doubling and counterfeiting, selling arms and the like. He would team up with robbers who would be arrested and brought up to him; he would order them to be locked up, only to release them again without bail.

In fact, anywhere else he would be in jail and not in the street checking crime or controlling those who checked crime. Only a country such as this which had reached the nadir of moral depravity would put him at the head of an organisation to check crime instead of being behind the bars.

3

His favourite drinking companions were delinquent Ibo traders, foreigners and tax-defaulting businessmen from whom he ceaselessly extorted bribes and drinks by threatening to have them locked up, their businesses closed down or they themselves deported, in the case of foreigners. He was always ready to threaten to contact Yaounde and report something to the Minister of Defence if he was not given what he wanted from anybody.

He was reckless by any standards, uncouth, immoral and wild. Yet, for all his recklessness he seemed to command a lot of respect in Yaounde. No complaint that was made against him seemed to affect his position as the Divisional Chief. In fact, it appeared that the more the people complained about him, the higher he rose in his job. It was generally known that he had gone to bed with all the attractive wives of his junior officers. If the husband protested, he was transferred to distance places. He could cause the release of any criminal or the arrest or imprisonment of even the most innocent citizen. He was above the law.

About two years before, when he was the assistant provincial Chief, the wives who had been his victims had led a delegation to Yaounde to protest to the Minister of Internal Security who had promised the severest punishment to him. The following year when appointments were made, he was appointed the Divisional Chief. Thereafter he was feared.

Because he was constantly in debt, and because Akroma did everything to ensure that each time Essomba brought a financial problem to him it was solved, there developed between the two men a rare bond of friendship. As though that was not enough, Akroma encouraged him to send his junior sister to the Lycee where the fees were virtually paid by Akroma.

It suited Akroma's purpose very well to know that the fate of people such as himself lay in the hands of nonentity. As far as the police were concerned, therefore, and so long as "Ninja" remained the boss in Nijombari, Akroma could not be easily arrested on any charge. He saw himself above the law.

Those who cared to know about his educational background knew that he had studied in the early seventies in the University of Legon in Ghana, and that he had worked for a long time in Ghana since completing the university. Upon returning to the country, so he gave people to believe, the Cameroon government had shown some reluctance in employing him and anybody else who studied in Ghana. Ghana, it was always remembered, was said to have harboured and encouraged terrorists and subversionists who went to study in Moscow in the sixties. This was common knowledge. Everybody called him Mula. In formal situations he was called *Monsieur Le Directeur* Fabian.

He was married to a Cameroonian girl from Kribi. But he married her not out of love or need, but convenience. He wanted to give his status respect so that whenever he attended a party he did so in the company of his wife. He never actually paid a dowry for the girl because he never went to Kribi to see her parents as she ceaselessly insisted. He instead invited the parents over to whom he gave some money and some gifts, none of which constituted a dowry. When they had their first child, Bonaventure, there was an unforgettable birth celebration. The Mayor of Nijombari was the Chairman, the Divisional Chief of Public Security was the M.C,. and the *Procureur de la Republique* was the Assistant M.C. In all, eight bottles of Champagne were opened. There were no less than 12 crates of Becks Beer, and numerous crates of other assorted drinks.

His wife came from the same village with Essomba, and so he wanted to cement his relationship with Essomba as well as make an impression on the public.

On his own part he never took the girl to his people as she also insisted. His case was clear: he was an orphan from Likomba in Tiko Sub Division. His father, the successor to their father's throne as Paramount Chief had been killed by the brother, his uncle. The same uncle had also killed his mother and before she died she had warned him never to set foot on the Likomba soil. She did not press the issue any more, since he provided for her needs without complaining.

Chapter Thirty-Four

(Saturday, March 23rd, 1986)

On Saturday morning, the day after Dangobert received the news of Reverend Akwa's death, Akroma paid an early visit to the *Commissaire* for Pubic Security, Mr. Mouralais Essomba. He found Essomba in uniform, drinking Schnapps and smoking a pipe, his eyes as red as palm oil. He may have slept with his uniform on because his shoes stank as if he had stepped into a pool of mud and had not bothered to take them off, clean and dry them.

The visit was prompted by two reasons. He wanted by some devious means, to know the extent of the investigations of the murder, to know the extent of the investigations of the murder. The second reason for coming through *Commissaire* Essomba who usually treats the most delicate problems with levity, into total distress.

"I have come this early to see you, *Monsieur Le Commissaire*," Akroma began, "because my school has also run into a problem."

"What problem. *Monsieur Le Directeur*? You know that your problems are mine."

"My driver was killed last night," he announced.

"How?"

2

Akroma was the only person who knew how J-P had died. If an autopsy were ever done on the corpse of Reverend Dieudonne. Akwa as well as that of J-P, it would be discovered that they were killed in the same manner. The assailant had sprayed a good quantity of Gas Lacrimogene into the face of the victim, causing the latter to collapse into unconsciousness. The victim had then probably been strangled in that state of unconsciousness. In the case f J-P, the murderer and himself had taken a late stroll down the deserted street. During that stroll they had discussed the possible consequences of Akwa's death on their future in Nijombari. The murderer had then smuggled the gas from his pocket and had sprayed it into J-P's face. The murderer had strangled J-P, dragged his lifeless body to the middle of the road and had escaped just in time before a vehicle showed up and discovered the body.

Even though he was the only witness to this crime, Akroma gave only the official version which he was doing well to propagate.

"Run over by a passing vehicle," he told *Commissaire* Essomba.

"Where?"

"In town in the branch leading to the church off the Commercial Avenue."

Commissaire Essomba had not recovered from the horrifying news when his phone rang. He walked to the corner of the house where the phone stood, picked up the receiver and said:

"*Commissaire* Essomba here, who is speaking?"

"Kum Dangobert," the voice said loudly.

"*Commissaire* Kum Dangobert?" Essomba inquired.

"In Charge of 19ème Arrondisement here in Douala," he said.

Akroma shuddered and looked round the house like a trapped rat. Had he walked into his own death? Would he have to kill Essomba too? Could he not jump out and escape from Nijombari and out of Cameroon?

"I am listening, *Monsieur Le Commissaire*," Essomba announced.

"This is an emergency and I would like you to treat it as such. It is also extremely important."

"Okay."

"Do you know the principal of College Classique Polyvalent No.1 de Nijombari?"

Essomba looked across at Akroma, cleared his throat nervously and answered.

"I know him," Essomba replied.

"What is his name?"

"That should be *Directeur* Njonjo Fabian Mula," he told him.

"Now, get this straight," Dangobert began very gravely. "That gentleman is a wanted man, for arson and manslaughter. He set a hotel on fire here in which a lady died. He is an illegal immigrant, a Ghanaian who should long have been deported. His true names are Patrickston Essuman Akroma.."

"Just a minute," Essomba said and looked across at *Directeur* Fabian again. The latter was listening and had therefore certainly caught that first bit of information. He was the subject of the call. The *Commissaire* suddenly decided to receive the rest of the information in his bedroom office.

Taking his drink with him he walked through the corridor into his bedroom where he picked the receiver and then continued.

"I am sorry", he said. "I wanted to continue this call in the room. I am listening."

"As I was saying," Dangobert resumed. "Right now, that gentleman is a prime suspect in the death of the Pastor that occurred there last night."

"Give me another second," Essomba said and then returned to the parlour to replace the receiver which he belatedly realized he had left lying on the side table, and through which he was now sure Akroma must have been following the whole talk. Essomba eyed Akroma malevolently as he returned to the room. There was guilt stamped indelibly on every nerve in Akroma's face.

"Go on, *Monsieur Le Commissaire*," Essomba resumed in his room.

"What I want done now," Dangobert went on, "is for you to put a watchful eye on that man. Do not alarm him, since he is unaware of our intentions. I do not see him as dangerous in any way. Just that we don't want to lose him. Make sure he does not leave town. We should be reaching Nijombari there in the evening. Get your boys to put an eye on him. Invite him for questioning and possibly detain him on a pretext. I leave here with my orderly by 5pm in my service vehicle. A deep blue Toyota jeep as usual, SN 3245X. I should be there at about eight."

"I'll keep in touch with you on my walkie-talkie as soon as you are within reach," *Commissaire* Essomba said.

"Do I come with my boys or yours will…."

"*Monsieur Le Commissaire*, to take away an unarmed civilian, you don't need a battalion. We should be able to do the job here. We will simply hand him over to you since you already had the case file. The rest of the paper work can be done later."

Commissaire Essomba did not drop the line. "We even have another problem on hand now, *Monsieur Le Commissaire*," he continued. "The driver of that man's school was killed late last night."

"That the driver is killed?"

"I just learned that a few minutes ago."

Dangobert nodded several times.

"How?" he asked.

"That he was knocked down by a passing vehicle late last night, or early this morning."

"It merely strengthens my guess," Dangobert said. "Let me tell you right away and without consulting any oracle that that your principal man has also killed the driver."

"How can that be, *Monsieur Le Commissaire*? For what reason?"

"Simple," Dangobert said. "Akwa recognised him, and when he killed Akwa he was certain that the only person who knew that Akwa knew him as the driver with whom he had been on the run all these years, was the driver."

Commissaire Essomba had wanted to inform Dangobert that he was right there in his house with the wanted man. But inadvertently, he dropped the receiver and the line went off. They were both unable to get across to each other again.

Chapter Thirty-Five

(Monday, March 24th 1986)

When the *Commissaire* returned to the Reception in his house where Akroma was sitting, he looked tired and confused. Akroma was his very good friend and one to whom he owed numerous favours.

Akroma knew that he was now being trailed.

"What's the problem, Patron?" he inquired, his chest rising and falling with fright, sweat rolling down from his brows as though he was undergoing some internal agony too severe to be voiced. And, in fact, he was in agony.

"No, something official," the man said after much hesitation and visible panic. "My boss called from Yaounde."

Then all of a sudden *Commissaire* inquired:

"Where did you tell me you actually came from?"

"Kumba. Why do you ask? Do you doubt it?"

"Not that I doubt it," *Commissaire* said

"Be honest with me, Patron, and tell me what is happening and I will tell you what you want to know."

The *Commissaire* scratched his head, sat up, tightened his lips and said:

"It is being suspected that you are not a Cameroonian."

"I am not, Patron," the man said with unusual candour. Since the whole truth was already known, there was no point hiding it. "I am a Ghanaian. I came here to try my luck."

"Then there is a serious problem. You have been caught."

"Caught, sir?"

"Yes," Essomba nodded. "I have been asked to arrest you and I'll go straight ahead to do so, if you do not buy your head."

Akroma sank into gloom and feverish despondency as he listened, head down.

"I don't want to be arrested," he said, "I will give you anything to help me to escape back to my country. Let me buy my head and go me safely. I beg you, for old friends' sake in the name of God."

Essomba reflected. He needed money to buy a plot and build a house. If he had enough money he could buy a house instead. He needed a private car which he could drive to his village. He needed money to drink with all the young girls about town, without belittling himself by forcing petty traders to give him a drink. And this was his opportunity!

"To escape from the net that I have been asked to throw over you," he told Akroma, "you need to give me personally two million francs."

"I can do that," Akroma said. "Even this night."

Commissaire Essomba smiled mischievously, inwardly regretting for not quoting a bigger figure. "I will also have to give my boss something if they begin to ask me questions about you," he said as an afterthought.

"From the two million?" Akroma asked.

"How from the two million?" Essomba asked. "We also suspect that you know the man who killed Rev. Akwa the other night, and also that you know why your driver had to die, even though you claim that it was a passing vehicle that knocked him down."

Akroma breathed in and out and shook his head.

"I can only tell you what I know to be true about myself. I have confessed that I am a Ghanaian. I have agreed to pay you 2 million francs so that you permit me to escape. I have agreed to add something for your boss. But for saying that I know anybody who killed those people, Sir, I say no. I am innocent and ignorant."

"Go for the thing, then"

Akroma stood at the door for a while and asked:

"What am I bringing for your boss?"

"The same thing," Essomba said.

As Akroma stepped out of the house Essomba thought it wise to go with him. Having been alerted, Akroma could go and never return. He drove Akroma in his service vehicle to the former's house where he brought the money in his brief case which he gave the *Commissaire*.

"Four million five hundred thousand francs." Akroma announced when Essomba looked at him questioningly.

"Four and half?"

Akroma nodded. "One good turn deserves another," Akroma said. He was not taking any chances. Essomba must be completely bought over!

The two men drove back to Essomba's office in the house where Akroma allowed the man time to count it. When he re-emerged he congratulated Akroma:

"You are a strong man," he said.

In the annals of criminal activity involving the police, the events that followed these words of congratulation would he historic.

2

"C*ommissaire*," Akroma called in a pained voice
"Anything?" Essomba inquired worriedly.

Akroma put his hand to his mouth for a second and said: "If you really want to save me, come in and let's sit down and think this thing over again."

Essomba felt his pistol, it was in place. That was enough warning that if Akroma was thinking of attacking him he was sure to lose. But how attack him, he asked himself, when he was in the process of saving him from arrest.

They went into Essomba's room.

"Tell me what you are thinking about," Essomba said.

Akroma reflected for just a few seconds and then began:

"I do not know what I have done to this man that he should leave all the criminals and murderers in Cameroon to test his knowledge of police investigation only on me. I just don't know."

Essomba smiled, "You don't know what you have done?" he asked.

"Well not that I don't know. There are hundreds of people doing what I am doing to survive. I do not understand why he should be following only me."

"Land", Essomba said.

"Land?"

"Yes, get to the point," Essomba told him.

Akroma took a very long time to reflect before saying:

"So long as this man lives, he will one day discover that it was you who allowed me to escape. And that will not be good for your record."

Essomba's mind was thrown into extreme turmoil. There seemed to be some sense in what Akroma had said. Akroma's desperate desire to escape and Essomba's prospect of getting rich at one stroke, blinded the two men to any reasonable calculations. The conversation that went on between the two men thereafter was not that between two human beings but between two reckless, lawless, wicked monsters in human form, and for whom human life counted for little, if their personal interests were at stake.

They would drive out of town and keep in touch with Dangobert by radio as he approached Nijombari. He, Essomba would keep the service vehicle out of sight, somewhere in the bush, but close enough to carry them back in a hurry to town. But it was Akroma to do it. It was a textbook rule in the police force that a police man should not shoot another police man,

Yes, Akroma would do it, but with Essomba's pistol. No problem whatsoever. Akroma had done three years of military service in the early seventies while still a student at Cape Coast University. Besides, even if he had not acquired any training, he needed only to be shown what to do and he would shoot himself into freedom. He would wear Essomba's discarded police uniform for the purpose.

"When the man from Douala comes here this evening," Essomba said, concluding the horrible plan, "we shall fight together to do away with him so that you go away without any trouble. I am the law."

Chapter Thirty-Six

(Monday, March 24th , 1986)

At precisely 7 o'clock Essomba's radio signalled there was a message. *Commissaire* Dangobert was as good as his word. He was 20 Kilometres away and would be in Nijombari itself in under thirty minutes.

In anticipation of the impending visit, and to ensure that his own elements did not interfere in the business and so embarrass him, *Commissaire* Essomba assigned his officers to command posts far away from the Douala –Nijombari road. Akroma and Essomba were at Eburakum, ten kilometres away from where Dangobert was talking, and an area which was generally dreaded by taxi drivers and clandestine drivers (popularly called *clandoes*), on account of the numerous police checks that took place around there. It was usually said amongst drivers plying that area that you could never have everything that the police wanted to see. This argument could be very easily substantiated by any of the drivers. They will tell you that as soon as the policeman stopped your vehicle he asked for the documents and then, even without looking at them asked you to park some twenty metres away. He then kept them while at the same time stopping some two, three, five or six other vehicles, from which he collected the same types of documents. He then casually went through the documents and decided to ask for what no driver could possibly be carrying.

For instance, he could ask for "a complete First Aid Box." This implied a medical kit that could take care of all possible emergency problems, ranging from compound fractures, nose bleeding and fainting fit to diarrhoea and dysentery. Quite naturally, no driver was capable of possessing all the necessary remedies. If you had all of these, you may need to produce a fire extinguisher. If you had one, you may to prove that it could put out a fire both on your own vehicle and that of another vehicle with which it had had a collision, and which did not carry one. It was a place transporters generally avoided just because they could never win against the police. Essomba had therefore chosen the right point for their operation.

2

Essomba followed him to the main road and helped him to mount a hasty road block – an old Indian bamboo on two stones, one on either side of the road. He then hurried back to his hideout with the radio glued to his ear. Five kilometres, four kilometres, three, two, one. As if God had blessed the occasion, not a soul passed by while they drove up to the place and mounted their road block. Not even a pedestrian. The headlights of a vehicle glowed against the evening sky from the Douala end of the road. Essomba spoke through his radio and confirmed that it was *Commissaire* Dangobert. He signalled to Akroma and then dashed into the bush.

Akroma was wearing Essomba's discarded Inspector's uniform and carrying the latter's automatic pistol As they had already planned, and as he was used to seeing policemen behave, Akroma flagged down the vehicle with his torch.

The jeep stopped, the lone occupant whom Akroma recognised very well wound down the glass to introduce himself. Akroma drew his gun and fired between the man's eyes. Unsuspecting, the stranger could not defend himself. The assailant immediately removed the road block and disappeared into the bush as originally planned, to meet his accomplice.

Essomba had not returned to the vehicle. He had stood some fifty metres away watching the execution of the plan. When the gun exploded, he shook as if fragments of the bullets had hit him. When they arrived the Eburakum spot, a faint moonlight shone through the thick clouds.

Immediately after the act, and as if to condemn the deed and foreshadow his doom, the faint moonlight disappeared. There then was heard a deep, chilling roll of thunder and a muttering of rising wind. Again, as though the shot had reached the heavens, a flash of lightning zipped through the sky. It had actually been drizzling when they got there, but they had been so engrossed in their crime that they had not noticed it. Now it began to rain.

The two men walked briskly away to Essomba's service car without saying a word to each other. When they got there, Akroma leaned on the driver's door holding his head down as if in bitter regret for what he had done.

Essomba tried to cheer him up.

"You should have been a policeman," he congratulated Akroma. "You did it as if you had been practising it all your life."

"Hmm" Akroma grunted. "I told you I was in the Cadet Corps for two years," he said deep down his throat, and then stood silent.

"Don't stand there looking like a child. God has already buttered your bread…." Essomba said from outside the driver's side.

3

Akroma heaved a sigh. The murder of Reverend Dieudonne Akwa and then of J-P, had not been followed by such pangs of remorse as he now felt. Guilt instantly metamorphosed into trepidation and acute insecurity. Could Essomba be trusted? The doubt began to rise in his morbid mind. Evidently there was telepathy at work because just then, Essomba slashed through his thoughts as though he had actually heard him voice them.

"Never mind, my friend," he said, "The only man to fear in this business right now is me. And I am on your side. All investigations will have to be carried out by me…"

Akroma's silence disturbed him. From the corner of his left eye he saw Akroma shake his head as a duck would do when it bathes in a pond.

The original arrangement was that immediately after the act Akroma would change into his own clothes which he had brought along with him He was then to go back to town and hire a vehicle from Mr. Yuta Calixt, a prominent businessman and a good friend of the duo. As soon as the hired vehicle left town Essomba was going to order his elements to make sure that no vehicle left Nijombari.

But Akroma thought differently. They say that those the gods would destroyed they first drive mad! Not only did he fear that Essomba could change his mind and kill him instead, he was no longer sure that he could trust Essomba to let him escape unmolested. The only way to escape unperturbed, therefore, was to keep Essomba out of his way- for good.

4

He looked over the bonnet of the vehicle. Essomba was still holding his head face down on his folded arms completely ignoring the rain that dripped on him through the canopy of rubber trees. He was listening without real awareness to the clamour of crickets all around him. Once a tree bat uttered a piercing spasm which reminded him of his now poignant anguish. Tears suddenly rose to his tired eyes and, mixing with the rain trickled down his cheeks. The weight of the deed on his heart had become too terrible for endurance. His future, unless strongly defended might well become a dry and windless desert in which he would wander, parched, and lost and full of exhaustion.

There were five bullets left in the gun. He made a slight sign which caused Essomba to lift his head. Impelled by the demonic force that had taken over complete control of him he shot Essomba in the right eye, shattering his entire face. Essomba uttered a loud groan slided down the side of the vehicle and collapsed.

Akroma climbed into the vehicle and shut the door. The rain, a thundering downpour now, seemed to be hurling itself at the window noisily, like pebbles tossed at the pane. He looked out lighting continued to crack through the sky. He waited for about twenty anxious minutes and then he climbed down, pulled Essomba over and searched him. There were five hundred thousand francs in his pocket. These he removed.

When he killed Dangobert he was still somehow himself. But the execution of Essomba transformed him into an outright phantom. He felt himself like a wingless bird that had just broken the branch of the tree on which it was perching, and which would now float and sink into the abyss below.

The gun just seemed to continue firing; bang! Bang! Bang! He placed his head on the steering wheel and plugged his ears. Perhaps it was the crack of thunder and not the shot of the gun. Perhaps it was both.

5

Akroma had long planned his escape. He did some banking in the course of the day. He caused BIAO Nijombari to transfer the sum of 21 million francs into his Lome account and had a receipt for the transfer before he left the bank. He kept 2 million francs to himself for his travel.

He would not even go to Yuta Calixt as originally arranged and hire a pick-up. With Reverend Dieudonne Akwa, J-P, Dangobert and Essomba dead, Akroma saw himself a free man. Having studied the Cameroonians legal system very closely, he did not see how he could be stopped. In his Inspector's uniform, he would drive to Douala before midnight. From Douala, using his Abessolo I.D. card, he would hire a taxi to Kumba. From Kumba he would hire a pick-up, jeep or any fast –moving vehicle to Mamfe and then to Ikok. Anybody looking for Njonjo Fabian would be wasting his time. At Ikok he would buy his way across the border to Nigeria. Once in Nigeria he would discard his Cameroonian I.D. cards and use his Ghanaian passport to return to Ghana, and land of freedom.

There was nothing, therefore, to stop him! With so many deaths in the hands of the police, he figured, there would be very much confusion. It should take a week or more for facts to be sorted out to the extent that he would be thought to be the wanted man. By that time he shall have long reached Ghana, the land of freedom. All being well that ends well, he thought.

When, after about twenty minutes he shook himself out of his reverie there was a milky film over his vision which gradually lightened gradually, bringing him face to face again with the grim reality of his heinous crime. His flaming eyes darkened further, the pallor of exhaustion having taken its toll on his face.

6

In his madness Akroma seemed to have taken too much for granted. Investigations into the causes of the deaths of Reverend Pastor Dieudonne Akwa and of driver Mombangui Jean-Paul could with some difficulty be eventually suppressed or misrepresented. With only a few threats the hotel attendants could have been told how to report the death of Akwa. With only a few guides those who found the body of J-P could have been forced to sing a different song.

There was so much Essomba could have said to Dangobert which would have made any further investigations into the two deaths unnecessary. And the matter would have died a natural death. Worse still, had Akroma unleashed his murderous instincts on an ordinary policeman, he would have used his money to exploit his relationship with Essomba and destroy the case files or make the crime less frightful. Had Akroma killed only Dangobert, it might have been possible eventually also, though not easy by any means, for Akroma to use his money to cause Essomba to find a way of covering him up.

In killing Dangobert, all Akroma knew was that he had finally put his mimesis to rest. But Dangobert was a *Commissaire*, a commanding officer! That in itself gave a terrifying dimension to the crime, the repercussions of which could not be easily imagined.

A slight incident emphasized this point. Not so long ago, in Douala, the principal of Lycee de Nilong, had complained to the police that a gang had made it a habit of gathering to smoke hemp in his playground late at night, an act which he said was affecting discipline in his school, since his students were gradually joining the rogues.

In response the *Commissaire* for Public Security dispatched a team of ten policemen one night. The gang was surrounded but a gunfight broke out. At the end four members of the gang were arrested. The gang leader shot his way into freedom, having mortally wounded a *Commissaire* in the process. The *Commissaire*, in turn, had wounded the gang leader in the ear. Two days afterwards, while the *Commissaire* was still receiving treatment on his deathbed, it was reported that the escapee had taken refuge in a private clinic where he was receiving medical attention. Five policemen walked into the clinic and gunned down the doctor and the nurse attending to the fugitive. In a ghoulish spectacle that ensued, all five policemen then proceeded to spray him with bullets from head to toe.

As if that was not enough, one of them took out a dagger and slashed the dead man beyond recognition in the face. As they walked away, one of the policemen gave what ought to have been taken as the unwritten law of the force. "Only the police has the right to shoot. You shoot a police we kill you one hundred times."

7

Akroma had not stopped at Dangobert. He had killed Essomba who was not only his arch-protector but also the protégé of the Minister of Defence. That was bound to unleash every iota of all the animal brutality with which the police force was generally associated. They would do anything to avenge the death of a colleague. The execution of two *Commissaire*s of Police would be received in Yaounde with horror, as a slap in the face, and would provoke a war in which money would have no place whatsoever.

Thus, while Akroma worked out his plans of escape and assembled money to buy his way into freedom, he hardly knew that he was as good as dead. The only good he could have done to himself should have been to hold the pistol to his own head and pull the trigger. He was unaware that as he sat in the vehicle a car drove up to the scene of the crime and, seeing what had happened, drove back towards Douala. He did not notice that another vehicle coming from Nijombari had also noticed the incident and returned to alarm the police. He was unaware that while he was still dreaming of his escape the police had been alerted both from Douala and Nijombari. He was unaware that Yaounde had already been contacted and that instructions had been given for Nijombari to be completely sealed off. He was unaware that even without receiving instructions from Yaounde the police, Gendarmes and military had already started acting without restriction, without responsibility, beating, raping, ransacking and pillaging, looting and killing.

The murder of two *Commissaire*s was tantamount to regicide. Even without finding out the exact perpetrator of the crime, it will be decided that Nijombari would not exist if she did not approve of the existence of the police. The pogrom that will be visited on Nijombari will remain the most blood-curdling of human atrocities ever registered. It was only a matter of time before they found Akroma frozen into immobility at the wheel.

The End